Praise for Mar

Marie Yates is an author and coach who works with survivors of rape and sexual abuse. She brings a very special expertise in writing *Reggie & Me*. A thoughtful and thought-provoking work of fiction, *Reggie and Me* is one of those deftly written novels that lingers in the mind and memory long after it is finished and set back upon the shelf. Very highly recommended for both community and academic library collections.
Julie Summers, Midwest Book Review

Reggie & Me is a heart-warming tale of survival after the most difficult of circumstances. Marie Yates has written a totally realistic and heart-rending story about the power of healing assisted by the love of a four-legged friend, filled with identifiable and inspirational characters that practically leap off the page.
Thomas E. Sniegoski, *New York Times* Bestselling author of *THE FALLEN* series, and the *BONE: QUEST FOR THE SPARK* trilogy.

Reggie & Me is an extremely inspiring 'must read' for any young person. The book offers a contemplation of the trials of teenage life, as the positive story carries its reader through the struggle of mastering them. We hope that Dani will inspire many other young people to take up our sport and improve their mental and physical wellbeing.'
British Taekwondo

Reggie & Me is a strong and courageous portrayal of a young girl's survival of rape. It is written from an autobiographical stance and it makes the book very real as a testimony of her survival, the style of language and expression is one representation of the parlance of young people themselves and I think this will make the book more 'appealing' and readable to this audience too. The strong feature of the book, which is particularly powerful,

is that Marie writes from the heart and with a young person's voice and her remarkable strength in her recovery may well be an inspiration to others as victims and those who can support a young person in this recovery.
Ruth Jones OBE, Director of the National Centre for the Study and Prevention of Violence and Abuse at the University of Worcester

I have already recommended *Reggie & Me* to a brave young woman and her mother who were both in need of support and understanding. I can imagine recommending it many more times. The book is written in an engaging style for young readers who need to know that they're not weird and they're not alone. I look forward to reading more about Dani and Reggie in the remaining books. I would encourage both professionals and parents who are supporting young people living with the impact of sexual abuse to introduce them to the Dani Moore Trilogy.
Dr Nina Burrowes, Psychologist, Speaker, Author

Frankie & Me

Frankie & Me

Marie Yates

LODESTONE
BOOKS

Winchester, UK
Washington, USA

First published by Lodestone Books, 2018
Lodestone Books is an imprint of John Hunt Publishing Ltd., No. 3 East Street,
Alresford, Hampshire SO24 9EE, UK
office1@jhpbooks.net
www.johnhuntpublishing.com

For distributor details and how to order please visit the 'Ordering' section on our website.

ISBN: 978 1 78535 772 5
978 1 78535 773 2 (ebook)
Library of Congress Control Number: 2017943743

A CIP catalogue record for this book is available from the British Library.

Design: Stuart Davies

Printed and bound by CPI Group (UK) Ltd, Croydon, CR0 4YY, UK

In memory of Stephanie Slater, who's courage to share her story of survival changed my life and to whom I will be forever grateful.

Other Books in the *Dani Moore Trilogy* by Marie Yates

Reggie & Me

FINALIST WINTER 2014/2015 THE PEOPLE'S BOOK PRIZE

(Lodestone Books, 978-1-78279-723-4)

Sammy & Me

(Lodestone Books, 978-1-78535-502-8)

One

I raced out of that cinema and didn't look back. It was halfway through the film, after a most incredible moment with Frankie, and I just ran. I haven't told her yet or replied to her message of 'WTF just happened? x.'

WTF did just happen? My grandma died. That's what happened.

In the cinema, I could feel my phone vibrating in my pocket. It wouldn't stop, which was weird because Mum never called when I was out, and I was with everyone else who might have been calling me.

I thought it was one of the girls having a joke, so reached for my phone and saw twenty-four missed calls from Mother Dearest. There was a text, which said, 'Please Come Home.'

My first thought was 'Reggie'. Why else would she be calling? There was an emergency, that much was obvious, and Mum was well enough to be using the phone so that left the only other being on earth that I loved more than life itself, my dog and best friend, Reggie.

I replied just saying 'on way' and I ran. I didn't want to talk on the phone, I didn't want to have to wait for her to pick it up, I wanted to get home and see Reggie.

My phone vibrated again in my pocket and, looking quickly, I could see messages from my friends:

Callie – oi, dude, what's up? x

Maya – Are you okay? Where'd you go? x

Katie – Call me, mate…what did Frankie do? x

That made me smile as I ran. What had Frankie done? She had done everything right and I'd run away. 'Reggie has to be okay, he has to be okay,' I repeated as I continued running all all the way home.

I'm ashamed to admit that as I burst through the front door

to be greeted by an excited, yet somewhat confused Reggie, the initial relief soon turned to anger as I could see Mum being comforted by her boyfriend Sammy, but I could also see that Reggie was absolutely fine. So, what had been so important that I'd needed to receive twenty-four missed calls?

'I was in the middle of the film.' The words came spilling out of my insensitive mouth in a tone that made Sammy mouth 'sit down' in a silent command. I sat, so did Reggie. I was impressed.

'Dani, thanks for coming home,' Mum said in a broken voice.

Okay, so that made me feel even worse. 'I had a call from your grandpa to tell us that your grandma died suddenly this morning.'

She burst into tears and I didn't know what to do. Sammy was comforting her, which I was pleased about as I couldn't move. I couldn't speak. My head was spinning with questions but nothing came out of my mouth. I was shocked, but I didn't cry. I looked to Reggie, who did his cute, quizzical head tilt, and smiled.

I smiled. I couldn't believe I'd smiled.

'Dani, are you okay?' Mum asked.

I created a new mantra of *don't look at Reggie, don't look at Reggie,* in my head. 'I don't know. She wasn't ill,' I helpfully pointed out.

Mum began to explain. 'Grandpa hasn't told me everything yet as he was obviously upset on the phone. The doctor said that she understands Mum – Grandma – was feeling unwell this morning and went back to bed. When Dad – I mean Grandpa – went up an hour or so later with a cuppa, she wasn't responding so he called the ambulance and kept trying to wake her up. In the rush, he forgot to take his mobile phone and couldn't remember our number, but Grandma never woke up, and they said at the hospital that there was nothing they could do. They thought it was a massive stroke.'

'Poor Grandpa, how is he?' I asked, but Mum couldn't answer.

She held out her arms for me to go to her but instead I reached for my phone to call him. He was on his own. I had never seen him on his own and I didn't think he'd know what to do without Grandma.

I saw the messages from my friends but didn't know what to reply. Grandpa wasn't picking up the phone, and Mum was crying and I had no idea what to do. A stroke? I'd learnt about strokes in a science lesson. I thought it had something to do with blood being cut off from the brain. Had it hurt? Had she been in pain? Had she known what was happening? I wished I had listened.

'Dani, we're going to need to pack a bag and go and stay with Grandpa to help sort everything out.'

I knew that was the right thing to do but every part of my body was screaming, 'I don't want to go.' I was worried I'd screamed it out loud as Mum said, 'I know you don't want to go, I know it'll be hard to go and stay there, but Grandpa needs our help. I'm their only child and I need *your* help.'

Once again, it felt as though she was reading my mind as she continued, 'I don't know how long we'll need to be there for, but work have said I can take the time I need to get everything sorted out and to go to the funeral.' She cried as she added quietly, 'I've never arranged a funeral before. I don't know what to do.'

'Don't worry,' Sammy said, 'the funeral director will talk you through everything and you can all make the decisions together.' For the first time since Sammy had come into our lives, I wished he was coming with us. He seemed to know what to say and what to do.

'Reggie's coming with us,' Mum said. 'Grandpa asked if he could come.'

The relief must have been obvious; my face never hid what I was feeling, and I instantly felt stronger. 'Okay, I'll go and pack our bags, mine and Reggie's,' I said, feeling I needed to explain.

What was I going to say to Frankie?

Two

I'm supposed to be packing. Instead, I've spent the last half an hour staring at the message from Frankie. I have so many things I want to say and I have no idea where to start.

I quickly type, 'Really sorry, my grandma died. Stuff going on here, will txt later. Sorry x.'

I guess that's a start. At least she knows I didn't run off because of what she said. Because of what we both said. That she likes me, and I like her.

We said that out loud. Well, she did, and I replied, but that still counts. I didn't see it coming at all and yet as soon as she said those words, 'You know I like you, right,' my whole world made sense. It was the most obvious thing to reply, 'You know I like you too, right.'

I felt my phone vibrating as we spoke. I didn't wanted to check it, but knew I had to.

What would have happened if I had stayed? I wish I could have. I feel bad even thinking that now.

Is this the pattern of my life, something amazing happens, so something horrible has to happen next? I had an amazing, easy life, and then I was raped and everything went horribly wrong. Then we adopted Reggie, which was the best day ever, and then I had the worst year at my new school, being bullied and feeling as if I would never get out of the black hole. I made friends, moved to sixth form and then Mum met Sammy, which, in fairness has turned out okay, but there were some really bad days when he was first around. I know that wasn't the worst thing ever, and maybe I could have been a bit nicer about the relationship, but it was tough. Now, I've had a moment where someone has actually said she likes me, and I have said I like her back, on the very day Grandma died. Maybe she's not happy that I like a girl. Nah, she died before Frankie said it.

I look at the text I sent to Frankie. I can't believe I wrote that. Why am I not crying?

As soon as I hear the beep, my heart leaps. 'Are you okay, hun? So sorry to hear the news, I'll see you really soon x.' Then my stomach sinks. It's Jane, not Frankie. Mum's best friend will always be someone I can count on, but she isn't the one I want to hear from.

Jane probably knows Grandma better than I do. I feel bad that I haven't thought about her. She's been Mum's best friend forever and must have spent half her childhood with my grandparents. This is a rubbish day for her too.

'Sad and shocked, but okay. Howz u? x,' I reply.

Jane is her usual philosophical self, which is to be expected. She can't switch off being a psychologist for a minute. 'Death is the only certainty in life, Dani. We have to make the most of every day and remember your grandma with a smile x.'

She knows how to make a crappy day even crappier. I know she's trying to make me feel better, but it hasn't worked. What if this is it? What if every good thing that that happens is followed by something horrible? Is it better to have an 'okay' life where nothing really great happens? Will that make the crappy days hurt less? I guess not.

I suppose Jane will come up with a reason for all this. 'Focus on the good stuff and remember that life is unfair sometimes,' she'd say in a professional way. What can possibly be good about Grandma dying? Nothing. Mum's crying, Grandpa must be heartbroken, and I might lose the one person who actually likes me. That's not Grandma's fault, but there's nothing good about this at all.

'I can't remember the last thing we talked about,' I say to Mum when she comes up to see how I'm doing.

'Me neither.' Mum smiles as she joins Reggie on the floor of my bedroom. He rolls over to make it clear he wants fuss and Mum happily obliges as we sit quietly, drinking our tea. 'Sammy's making us something to eat and then we'll get going if that's okay with you?'

Reggie hears the words 'get going' and thinks that means something much more exciting than what is actually going to happen. 'Good idea,' I say to him and get up to take him out.

'The fresh air will do us all good,' Mum says, and she stands. 'Let's leave Sammy to the cooking and have a quick walk.'

That's it. Mum has said the 'w' word and the atmosphere has changed immediately. No amount of crying or sadness can get in the way of smiling at an excited Reggie when he hears the word 'walk'.

Walking together through a quiet park, we play with Reggie and talk about what we need to pack.

Getting our stuff together will be easy, but the amount of kit Reggie needs usually means there won't be much space left for our bags. Having a big dog means he also has a big bed, needs big towels to prevent a big mess, and needs a big bag of food. There's the big bowl for the big food and big toys to keep him occupied. The back of our car will be filled with everything he needs with our bags squished wherever there is room. We won't have it any other way and I think we are both relieved he is coming with us as a distraction from what is happening.

'It's not going to be easy, but we'll figure out how to deal with it,' Mum says, and she puts her arm around me. 'We always do.'

Three

'Will you please put that phone away!' Mum had become increasingly annoying the closer we had got to Grandpa's house last night. It had been a long drive and I'd spent most of it staring at my phone, wishing Frankie would reply.

She still hadn't by the time we arrived and after some hugs and tears were sitting in the living room looking at each other.

Frankie must have seen the message. Why wouldn't she reply? Had I upset her so much that she wasn't even going to talk to me about Grandma dying? I felt my head was going to explode. It wasn't the best situation I'd ever been in. Mum was upset, Grandpa was sitting in his chair, staring at Grandma's empty chair, and it was my job to keep Reggie off their sofa, well, his sofa now I supposed.

He was allowed on the sofa at home so it made total sense to him that all sofas were designed especially for him to stretch out on. Grandpa said he didn't mind.

'Mum never liked him going on the sofa,' my mum replied, and then cried.

I decided it would be my mission to make him love lying on his bed instead. Armed with his favourite treats and his favourite toys, I made sure that his bed was better than the sofa.

It was all going well until Grandpa's friend came over, sat down and tapped on the sofa as he called out, 'Come here, mate. Come and have some fuss.'

Reggie ran over and happily obliged. Grandpa winked at me as Mum stormed off to the kitchen muttering, 'What's the point?'

At least something made Grandpa smile. I was relieved he was watching Reggie make a new friend and not staring at Grandma's chair.

Grandpa's friend had lost his wife a couple of years before too, and I felt awkward being there as they started talking. Mum was washing up and still muttering, so I escaped to my room for the rest of the evening.

People say that staring at your phone doesn't make it beep. They're wrong. They obviously didn't stare at it for long enough, like I have all day.

'So soz, babe, my battery died, r u ok? x.'

I breathe out for what feels like the first time in hours. Frankie has replied. She doesn't hate me. She called me babe, what does that mean? Wait, she always calls me babe. She doesn't hate me.

Before I have a chance to start replying, the phone beeps again. 'Shit, soz, shouldn't have said died, really soz x.' Yep, she really doesn't hate me.

Frankie must be with the others as my phone is beeping away with condolences. My friends have been worried about me and it feels like a lifetime ago that we were sitting in the cinema rather than twenty-four hours ago.

It feels like my life is a million miles away. Being back here, just down the road from our old house, is not where I want to be. I haven't been outside yet.

Mum was up this morning and took Reggie out before I had the chance because she knew I didn't want to see anyone from 'before'. It wasn't far from here that I was raped on my way home from school.

Also, it was dark when we drove here last night, and I noticed that Mum had taken a two-mile detour to get to Grandpa's. She said she might 'pop to the shop' but we both knew it was closed and she reached out and touched my arm as we turned right, instead of left, which would have taken us past that place.

I should be thinking about Grandma now, about how I can help Grandpa, and how I can help Mum with all of the organising. Instead, I'm hiding away in my room. Being back here has made me question what happened with Frankie. Do I really like her? I don't know if it's real or if I'm too scared to like a guy because of what happened. I've never fancied a guy, but I was only fourteen when I was raped. Then, I was never that interested when my old friends were talking about boys they liked. I haven't met any boys I like since then either, not in 'that' way. Nobody liked me when I moved schools and, since I've been in Sixth Form, I've found the guys are quite annoying and I've been hanging out with the girls. How do I know if I can trust my feelings? There are guys I train with at taekwondo, but they're just mates and I have a laugh with them. They're nice, but I never felt the same way when they touched me as I did when Frankie touched my hand in the cinema. Admittedly, the guys at taekwondo were usually about to kick me in the head, but I don't think that would have made a difference.

I've never really thought that I might be gay, but I've never really thought I might be straight either! I haven't thought anything. The two people in my life I look up to are Mum (not that I'd tell her) and Jane (not that I'd tell her either). One's straight and one's gay so it has always been part of life and no big deal. I know that neither of them would care, in the nicest possible way, but I care. I don't want to mess Frankie around and I want to be able to trust my feelings, whatever they might be. I don't want to hurt Frankie if it turns out that I'm actually just scared of being with a guy because of what happened to me.

'Father Carl's here,' calls the voice of my agitated mother. This is an instruction to go downstairs and not just information. I suppose the arrival of a Catholic priest is a sign that I should stop thinking about how much I might like Frankie. Might? Who am I kidding? I do like her, a lot. I just need to make sure it's for the right reasons.

For now, I need to try to remember Grandma's favourite hymn. I only remember her singing, 'I'll Never Fall in Love Again,' by some old guy called Burt. I guess that's true for her now.

Four

Once I started crying, I couldn't stop.

I'd never been to a funeral before so I had no idea what to expect. Everyone was gathering outside and quietly talking to each other as if normal volume was against the rules – rules that nobody had shared with me. I hadn't thought about the other people who'd be there; people I'd never met who had been friends with Grandma for years, people who were now chatting to Grandpa and saying how sorry they were. Why did people say 'sorry'? It wasn't like it was their fault she'd died.

'It's nice to see you, Dani, although I'm sorry it's under these circumstances.' I spun around to find one of my old teachers standing in front of me. My first thought was, 'Wow, she's shorter than I remember,' until I quickly came to my senses and realised I was older and taller than when I'd last seen her. At that time she had walked past me in the corridor of my old school and hadn't made eye contact. Even though she had taught me for two years, clearly she'd had no idea what to do or say when I'd returned to school after what had happened. Talking to me today, she still seemed uncomfortable.

'How are you getting on in your new school? Are you still in school?' she asked.

'Of course,' I said, a little too defensively. 'It's amazing, I'm in Sixth Form now and I love it.' I stopped myself, realising I was too loud for the current gathering of people.

'That's great to hear and I'm pleased to see you looking so well, you know, after everything.'

She didn't know the half of it. She walked away, leaving the word 'everything' hanging in the air.

What a great reminder, I thanked her for that.

What does she expect me to look like? I wasn't a quivering wreck last time she saw me as far as I remember, not that she actually looked at me. Considering my grandma has just died, would it be weird if I did look like a quivering wreck? No, I don't think so.

I was having this silent rant in my head while my face was obviously giving away how I was feeling. I felt Mum's arm guiding me over to the door of the church and we were ushered into the front bench by an old woman clutching hymn books. 'Number 427,' she said, as she handed us a book each.

'What's number 427,' I asked.

Grandpa turned to me, his tired face looking defeated, yet thoughtful. 'That's the number of people who've had funerals here this year. Grandma is number 427.'

'What?'

'It's the hymn number, Dani, just open your book,' Mum said. 'Dad, there's a time and place.' She was not impressed. Grandpa winked at me and I had a sudden urge to laugh. I hadn't thought much about the afterlife or what I believed might happen when you died. I definitely hadn't imagined it to be like the cheese counter at a supermarket where someone called out your number and you got...well, I wouldn't know what you'd get, but I reckoned it had to be better than cheese.

The most horrendous noise shattered my thoughts of the great cheese counter in the sky. Hymn number 427 was being destroyed by an old woman playing the organ. I looked around and everyone was mumbling the words into their hymn books. The doors of the church opened and in walked Father Carl, closely followed by stern looking men carrying Grandma's coffin on their shoulders.

That's when it hit me. Grandma was in the coffin, she wasn't coming back. I would never see her again. Mum wouldn't see her mum again and poor Grandpa would never see the woman he loved again.

I cried.

I cried as Father Carl talked about how wonderful Grandma was. I cried as Mum stood up and talked about how lucky she was to have been raised by such a fantastic woman. I cried as the old woman destroyed another two hymns at full volume. I cried because it hit me that I'd never see Grandma again. But I realised I was mostly crying because Grandma had never heard Mum say those words. It wasn't like they were the best of friends. Grandma had said some unforgivable things to Mum in the aftermath of the attack. If Mum really felt the things she had just said out loud to this group of people, then why hadn't she made more effort to spend time with Grandma when she was alive? It was not like she'd stand up at a funeral and say, 'Actually, she's been a bit of a bitch over the last couple of years,' but if she meant it when she'd said that she loved her mum and was grateful for everything she'd taught her, why didn't she tell her? Maybe she thought she'd have more time.

'Did Grandma know you felt that way?' I asked as we walked back out of the church.

'I hope so, just as I know you love me even when you're angry or hurting because we hurt the people we're closest to.'

'That's silly,' I said, still crying. Mum handed me over to Jane so that she could go and talk to people. I was relieved that I didn't have to make small talk with strangers. Jane put her arm around me and walked me to her car, handing me a packet of tissues. We sat in silence, watching as random strangers came to shake Mum's hand and tell her that they were sorry. Everyone was sorry.

'Christ, that music probably finished off at least two more old people,' Jane said, and we both dissolved into laughter, hopefully far enough away that nobody could hear us.

Five

It has been a really rubbish week but finally being back at home has made everything seem better. I don't want to experience another funeral for a very long time. The only good thing, if you can call it that, was when I spoke to some of Grandma's friends at the wake.

I was surrounded by people sharing stories of Grandma in her youth, and before she had Mum. The stories made her sound like someone I would have wanted to have been friends with. She had broken the rules, had always been in trouble, but only because she had been standing up for what she had believed in.

'Your grandma was sent home from school in disgrace on the first day of term one year,' shrieked one of her friends. 'She decided that it wasn't fair the boys could wear trousers and yet the girls had to wear skirts; it was cold and we weren't able to afford tights. Well, she marched into class, proudly wearing her brother's trousers and was promptly marched to the headmaster's office and then marched off the premises. She was all mouth until the school called her father and she was back, wearing a skirt, before the morning milk break.'

They laughed as they shared stories and I learnt more about my grandma in that one hour than I had done throughout my whole life. That made me sad as I had seen her as an old woman, not a woman with a whole lifetime of stories.

The wake meant that I enjoyed some time with Grandpa, and I figured he must have some cool stories too.

We walked Reggie, we talked and I found out that he'd proposed to my grandma over fish and chips. 'That's as romantic as it got in our day.' He smiled. 'And it worked. She said, "yes".' He admitted that he'd never spoken ill of my biological father but had 'always hated that muppet'.

'You don't need him in your life, Dani,' he said. 'He'd promise you the earth and break your heart, like he did to your mother.'

'I don't want to meet him, so don't worry, I won't be looking.' I decided a while ago that my biological father was of no importance to me whatsoever. He didn't want to be in my life so I wasn't going to waste my time worrying about it.

'Your mum's finally got a good'un now, hasn't she?' That was the first time I'd heard Grandpa mention Sammy. 'It's good to know she's being looked after.'

I hadn't thought about it like that. Mum hadn't had someone to look after her for a long time. She had Jane, but that wasn't the same thing.

Sammy was there when we got home. He'd made dinner and cleaned up. Grandpa was right – she did have a 'good'un'.

I was worried about Grandpa being on his own once we were home. His parting words had been, 'It's okay, Dani, I'll be all right even though there's nobody to nag me. I can watch the football in peace,' which should have dispelled my fears.

'We'll see him soon,' Mum assured me, and when I called him to tell him we were home, I was certain I could hear the sound of a football match in the background.

I'm now hiding away upstairs as Jane and her girlfriend, Lucy are here for a couple of days before Mum goes back to work. They're downstairs with Mum, Sammy, and wine, embarrassing each other with stories about how they got into trouble as kids and how Grandma would always find out. I've heard it all before. Lucy has promised me that she won't drink too much so she'll be ready to help me with some taekwondo training tomorrow. She's a black belt and I'm in awe of her skills. I'm working towards my red belt and have missed my grading because of being away. I explained to my coach why and he said that if I worked hard and was ready for the grading, he'd arrange for me to do it due to the circumstances. He said it would give me a focus and I wouldn't have to wait another three months. That was really kind of him and I don't want to let him down. I haven't been training while I've been away and I've missed it. Having Lucy here means that I can get some expert coaching and be ready for my grading. She's promised to help me in the morning and that'll keep me occupied as I am meeting up with Frankie tomorrow afternoon.

I texted her yesterday to tell her we were coming home. 'Oh, babe, I'm back in the land of doom, wish I could be with you x,' she replied. My heart skipped a beat and I wished I could be with her too.

She's back visiting friends where she used to live. She called it the 'land of doom' because 'it's the most backward village in the country where broadband is slower than a dolphin on land and the people are still wearing shell suits.' I had to google what a shell suit was and I was glad Frankie hadn't brought that look to Sixth Form.

Now that we're about to meet up, I feel nervous. We're going back to Sixth Form next week, I have my taekwondo grading, I need to think about applying to Uni, which Jane has reminded me about for the millionth time, and I have much work to catch up on after the last couple of weeks. Thinking about Frankie – about how I feel, and about what I want – is taking up 99 per cent of my time. I even dreamt about her last night. We were back at the cinema, without the others, and she kissed me. I woke up wondering if that was what had happened, then wished that *was* what had happened. Now I'm back to not knowing what I want. It's exhausting being me.

For now, I feel like the only grown up in the house. I'm going to bed while the adult-children are making a lot of noise downstairs!

Six

I'm getting ready to see Frankie. A morning of taekwondo definitely took my mind off my nerves about seeing her again.

Lucy was so good and I struggled to keep up with what she was showing me. She was explaining the theory while slowly doing the movements; and even though it made total sense as she was doing it, my brain and body weren't able to translate it into action. She was really nice to me and didn't make me feel like an idiot for not getting it. We went right back to basics and did moves from each of the gradings I'd already passed.

'You're really good. A natural,' Lucy told me when we went back to the first grading I'd ever done.

'I should be able to do this, it's for beginners,' I replied, less than impressed although grateful I could remember.

'If you don't have the foundations, how will you be able to improve and develop?'

Okay, so she had a point and doing all of the basic exercises reminded my brain and body what I was doing. I didn't feel like I was failing and didn't feel frustrated that I couldn't do the hardest moves to begin with.

'Let's try again, slowly,' Lucy instructed as she took me through the movements and explained what each stage was for.

'That makes sense now,' I tried to say, but I was out of breath and was realising how much work I had to do to be ready for my grading. 'I'm knackered.'

'One more time and we'll leave it for today.'

I did it, I needed to get faster, but I did it. That was the first time I'd been able to get that right and it felt really good. 'Thank you, I never thought I'd get there,' I wheezed, trying to stand upright and failing miserably.

'Practice makes perfect is a crappy saying, but it's true. If you do that four or five times a day until your grading, you'll nail it.'

I didn't mean to, but I rolled my eyes. I'd heard that a thousand times before. I knew it was true and I knew it was what I needed to do. I just tended to lose motivation. I really wanted to pass my grading, yet day by day, I didn't want to practice.

'It won't be handed to you on a plate,' Lucy said, which convinced me that every adult had some sort of mind-reading ability. 'It's what you do behind the scenes that allows you to have those two minutes of glory and pass that grading with flying colours. I know you want to be good at this – you are good at this, but to be better than good, you need to put the hours in.'

'They sound like wise words,' Jane said as she came through the door. 'We need to head off now, wise one,' she joked. I saw the time. I'd been so engrossed in training that I'd forgotten it.

Thanking Lucy again, I raced to the shower. Jane shouted, 'We'll be off then, you must be seeing someone special to run off without saying goodbye.'

'I'm just late, see ya,' was the only reply needed for Jane to know that she was right. Almost as soon as the front door shut my phone beeped.

'Have fun and don't do anything I wouldn't do x.' OMG, did she know about Frankie? How could she know? She couldn't know. Nobody knew.

Jane's text is still on my mind when, after saying goodbye to Reggie, I walk into town to meet Frankie. Meeting at the coffee shop is a standing joke as neither of us like coffee but it's where everyone from Sixth Form goes.

As I walk in the door I see Frankie is already sitting at a table. I sit down opposite her.

'I've missed you,' Frankie whispers, and hugs me. 'I wish I could've been around to cheer you up, I'm sorry you've had a shitty time.'

'It hasn't been all bad,' I admit. 'I've been looking forward to seeing you.'

Frankie has already ordered for me. Sitting with our hot chocolates in coffee mugs, we talk about what we've been doing, about Grandma and about Frankie's visit to the 'land of doom'. Neither of us knows what to say about what happened at the cinema. I don't know if I should bring it up and Frankie isn't saying anything.

We go quiet, and no doubt we are both thinking the same thing.

'Dude, are we going to sit here like it never happened?' is Frankie's subtle way of dealing with the situation. She is her usual loud self and I find myself looking around to see if anyone is listening. 'Is there someone else you'd rather talk to?' she says in response to my visual sweep of the coffee shop.

'Of course not. I'm just not sure what to say,' I answer. I genuinely have no idea what to say or do. I can feel my stomach doing funny things, I can't look Frankie in the eye, and while I want to run out of the coffee shop at the speed of light, there is also nowhere on earth I'd rather be. Is this what it's supposed to feel like?

'It's all cool, we like each other, that's a good start,' Frankie reassures me. 'Let's chill out and hang out today and we don't have to talk about anything.'

'Sounds good,' I reply, and then can't think of anything else to say. My mind goes blank and I find myself staring at the bottom of my empty mug. I have to be honest. Where do I start with that? 'I guess I just need some time to think. The last couple of weeks have been the best and the worst all at the same time.'

'As long as I'm defined as the best, we're all good.' Frankie laughs. 'Shit, sorry, I've done it again. It's not like a funeral would be the best, unless you didn't like your grandma? Shit, sorry. I'll shut up.'

'Yeah, in comparison to my grandma's funeral, you're the

best thing that's happened over the last couple of weeks.' I laugh. Thankfully, we are both laughing again, and the awkward silence is behind us.

Seven

Back to reality. After the summer holiday I've just had, I thought going back to Sixth Form would be a break. I don't think that anymore.

This morning, I couldn't figure out where the annoying tune was coming from. I recognised it, but it had been so long since I last heard it that I had forgotten what it was.

'Turn that bloody alarm off,' was the morning greeting from Mum who was shouting from downstairs. The smell of burning toast drifted into the room. 'Will you get up? Have you forgotten where you're going today?'

I couldn't bring myself to shout back down the stairs and the smell of burnt toast wasn't making me want to join Mum for breakfast. After attempting to wake myself up with a cold shower and then succeeding in waking myself up by stubbing my toe on the bathroom door, I was almost ready.

I only had two lessons timetabled for the day and even that felt like too much of an effort.

'U up? See ya soon x,' came the first message of the day from Frankie. That message turbocharged my morning; I was dressed and shovelling cereal before Mum could tell me once more that I was running late.

'Have a good day,' she shouted. I grabbed my bag and, shutting the front door, started the walk to Sixth Form.

A text came in from Katie. 'This is the beginning of the end x.' We hadn't seen each other for ages. She had been my lifeline at secondary school and had introduced me to Callie and Maya, who had kept in touch and were really nice to me while I was away with Grandpa. Katie was totally preoccupied with her boyfriend, Cal, so I didn't know if I would see her today.

'Bring it on x,' I replied.

Just as I thought about my friends, my phone went off again in my pocket.

'Back 2 skool, loser. Ready 4 ur tattoo yet? x,' Callie messaged. Ever since she decided to abandon us at Sixth Form and go to Art College she had been following her dream of becoming a tattoo artist. She was going to be amazing, and I reckoned she'd be world famous, but I was waiting until she'd had a lot more practice before she took the gun to my skin.

'Almost ready, as soon as you win your first award, you can have my arm. x.'

'I don't wanna do this x,' was Maya's plea to the Universe.

'I have cake x,' I lied, but I knew it would make Maya smile. She was one of the calmest, gentlest people I'd ever met. Hanging out with her made me feel like everything was going to be okay, even when she didn't say anything, or when she sent messages like that. I knew she would have done all her work and would be at the first lesson five minutes early, no matter what she said.

Katie was right, it was the beginning of the end. Jane had dropped a few hints about thinking about the future and deciding whether or not I wanted to go to Uni. It was only because of everything that had been going on that she had let it go over the summer. Bang on cue there was the text I knew would come from her: 'Good luck, kid. Work hard, this is a big year for you. x.' It wouldn't be long until she started on her lectures too… 'You need to think about what you want to do with your life. You're too smart to stand in your own way. You can be anything you want to be.' That would be great, if only I knew what I wanted to be. I still thought I wanted to be a Sports Psychologist, but might need to be better at sport…and psychology!

I was sure I'd figure it out. Today, I just needed to see Frankie, catch up with my friends, and then stay awake for two lessons. That was also the order of priority!

My heart skipped a beat as I heard, 'There you are, I've been waiting.' Frankie touched my arm as she said it and my whole body tingled.

I managed a pathetic, 'Hey,' and looked around to see if anyone had noticed that my face had turned bright red. At least, that what it felt like.

'Who are you looking for,' she asked, and I felt silly.

'Just Maya, we're meeting up for the lesson,' I lied. Lying is not something I do well and I was convinced my face was so red that it would blister at any minute.

'Cool, well have fun and I'll see you in an hour.'

We both knew that Maya would already be sitting outside the classroom door, which was exactly where I found her two minutes later. We went into class together.

I was so totally preoccupied I didn't hear a word that she said. After a whole summer of not seeing her I felt bad, she deserved better than that. I wasn't going to turn into Katie and ignore my friends because I'd found someone I liked. At least, I didn't want to turn into Katie.

Sitting through the hour of psychology with Maya, all I could think about was seeing Frankie at the next lesson. Then, when I got to the next lesson, I felt awkward and wanted to go home.

Thinking about it now, I can't spend my final year of Sixth Form like this and I'm pretty sure that Frankie's getting annoyed with me too. I had no problem talking to her before we said those words. She's the same person. I'm the same person, and yet everything feels completely different.

I think my friends know how I feel, but if I talk to them, I'm scared I'll be talked about. I can't face another year of people talking behind my back. That final year of secondary school was the worst year ever and I can't do it again. Maybe things should go back to how they were before that night at the cinema. Life was much simpler then.

Eight

'That thing is an extension of your hand, do you ever put it down?' mutters Grandpa.

I quickly text Frankie to say I'll be stuck at home all day. 'I've been instructed to be here for dinner x,' I write.

'Gutted x,' she replies, and I want to text back 'me too', but that would be a lie.

I was almost relieved when Mum had said that Grandpa was going to be staying for the weekend and she wanted me to spend some time with him. I shouldn't need an excuse not to see Frankie, should I?

The fact that Grandpa has started to annoy me after only half an hour this morning almost makes me rethink going out this evening, but I know he's having a rough time. It must be so hard, losing the person who has been by your side for so many years.

'We need to be patient,' Mum said earlier, and then screamed into a tea towel. That was after only ten minutes, so I'm doing quite well with my half hour.

Grandpa isn't the easiest man to be around and he has a tendency to follow us around, which neither of us are used to.

I go to join Mum who is making tea in the kitchen and he appears in the doorway. I'm just preparing Reggie's breakfast when he comments that Reggie doesn't seem to like him anymore. 'Let him eat, and then I'm sure he'll love you again,' I say with as much patience as I can manage, but sounding a bit snappy.

'All right, I'll go and be quiet somewhere else,' he mumbles, and he shuffles off back to the living room. Two minutes later, he's back. 'I can't find the mugs and I'm gasping for a cuppa.'

I also need to carry a tea towel around with me to scream into. Mum soon finds a reason to 'pop to the shop' and I wish I had thought of that. I do have an essay to write.

'Come and sit with me,' Grandpa says with noticeable sadness in his voice.

I feel awful. The essay can wait, although it doesn't take much for me to decide an essay can wait. At least when we are sitting together in the living room he isn't appearing in doorways. Reggie settles with us, which is a relief as Grandpa doesn't seem to understand how much sick a dog of his size can create if he plays on a full stomach. Mum has managed the longest 'pop to the shop' in the history of 'popping to the shops' and I will admit that I'm thinking about Mum owing me a favour or two for babysitting Grandpa because she has bailed out.

'Your grandma was very proud of you, you know.'

I instantly feel bad about silently listing all the things I am planning to ask Mum for.

'I wish I'd got to know her better. Her friends told me stories about her that made her sound really cool.'

'She would've liked to have been described as cool.' Grandpa laughs. That is the first time I've heard him laugh since we found out Grandma had died. 'She was a trailblazer in her day. A cool trailblazer. All of the things you take for granted, she had to fight for.'

He doesn't say that in a patronising way, he says it with pride and he's right. I have never had to fight to wear trousers! Well, maybe once when Mum tried to make me wear a dress for a wedding, but that's not really the same thing. The fight hadn't lasted long. I remember my full-on tantrum being effective and Mum throwing my 'smart' trousers on the bed and then trying to find the iron to sort out my 'smart' top.

'She had to fight to marry me too.'

'Why? What was wrong with you?' The words come tumbling out of my mouth before I have a chance to stop them. Luckily, Grandpa laughs.

'I didn't think there was anything wrong with me and neither did your grandma. Her father didn't think I was good enough. I was a milkman in the mornings and a window cleaner in the afternoons, trying to save enough money for our first home. He thought she could do better.'

'She probably could have,' I whisper to Reggie, and Grandpa agrees.

'We made each other laugh, she was my best friend.' We sit quietly, watching Reggie as he stretches in his sleep and settles against my leg. He is always the perfect distraction and allows us to sit in silence without any awkwardness.

'You remember that, Dani. You can't go wrong if you marry your best friend, someone who makes you laugh and makes your heart skip a beat every time you see them.'

My eyes shoot to the floor and my face turns the colour of my strawberry Ribena.

'There's someone special, isn't there? If you won't tell me who it is, I'll have to ask Reggie, I know you tell him everything.'

I panic for a second and then remember that my secrets are safe with my boy. Doh! 'I don't know, but if I can be as happy as you and Grandma were, then I'll be lucky.'

'Yeah, yeah, good answer. Does that mean you're not going to tell me who they are?'

'Nope!'

He said 'they'. He didn't say 'he' or 'she'. That's weird, or is it? I don't know.

'Well, whoever they are, they'll be lucky to be with you, and if they ever hurt you, send them my way.'

That makes me smile. The thought of Grandpa trying to catch Frankie, the superstar runner, when he struggles to get to the kitchen without a rest would be something worth watching.

'Are you two okay?' Mum says when she finally makes it home. She's bought cake so all is forgiven.

'Actually, yeah, we're really good,' I tell her, and mean it.

Nine

After a quiet birthday over the summer in the midst of everything that was going on with Grandma, Mum surprised me this morning. I heard her and Grandpa laughing downstairs which was weird in itself and went downstairs to join them for breakfast.

'We have something to tell you,' Mum announced as she handed me my mug of tea.

Why do I always panic when I hear something like that? Even though both Mum and Grandpa were smiling, I still thought I'd done something wrong and was about to get a roasting.

'Your grandma wouldn't have wanted you to miss out on your birthday because of her,' said Grandpa as he handed me a card.

'What's this?' I asked, even though I could clearly see it was a card. My eyes began to fill up with tears as I saw her writing on the envelope.

'We didn't give it to you at the time as we wanted you to be in a happier place so you could enjoy it.'

There was me thinking Grandpa had forgotten my birthday. I knew that he wasn't in charge of birthdays and that it was Grandma's job to buy the presents and write the cards. He had said 'Happy Birthday' but I knew that Mum had prompted him and I didn't think much more of it while there were so many other things going on.

'This is something your grandma, and grandpa, wanted to give you for your seventeenth and I couldn't stop them,' Mum said, becoming tearful.

They must have been talking about this before Grandma died. None of them had any idea that I'd be opening the card without Grandma being there to see my reaction. In that moment, I missed her. I really missed her. We all did.

'Open it,' Mum and Grandpa said in unison.

'YES!' They were as pleased with my reaction as I was with my present. 'Driving Lessons!' I shouted. 'That's awesome, thank you so much.'

'Keep reading,' said Mum impatiently.

'TODAY?' I reached a pitch that made Reggie tilt his head at almost ninety degrees and then sat staring at the card. Grandma had written that they were paying for a course of driving lessons for me and in Grandpa's scrawl, below it, was written, 'The first lesson is booked, so we'll all be staying off the roads at 3pm today.'

'Your grandpa wanted to be here to wave you off on your first lesson and laugh as you bounce up the road,' Mum said, beginning to look a little bit nervous.

'Thank you so much, I can't wait.' I looked up and mouthed the words, 'Thank you, Grandma,' hoping that somehow, she'd know how grateful I was.

First things first, I wanted to text Frankie. My first thought was that I wanted to tell her my news, but something stopped me. I hadn't heard from her since yesterday and I still hadn't replied to her message. Should I tell her or not?

I raced upstairs for a shower and to get ready for what was turning out to be a much better day than I could have imagined. There was a knock at my bedroom door and Mum came in with a look on her face that meant a 'serious' talk was coming.

'It's okay, I'll be safe, I won't crash into a house or drive through a red light,' I joked.

'Danielle,' Mum said, and I knew she meant business as I had been fully named. 'Sit down for a minute.'

I hadn't heard that tone of voice in a while, and I knew that we would be talking about something I didn't want to talk about.

'I spoke to Jane about how to make these lessons as safe as possible for you.' *Yep, here we go.* 'We have arranged for a female instructor as I know that being in a small space with a stranger isn't easy. You won't be able to use your phone while you're driving, but if you feel uncomfortable at any point, just pull over, stop the car and call me.'

'There's a strong chance you're over-thinking this,' I replied, 'but thanks for booking a female instructor.'

I hadn't even thought about it. That had to be progress! I was so excited by the thought of learning to drive I hadn't thought about being in a car with an instructor or whether that instructor would be a man or a woman. If a man had turned up, I might have freaked out a bit, so I was pleased that it was to be a woman, but I was even more pleased that it hadn't been the first thought I'd had. A year ago, I think I would have immediately worried about who I was about to get in a car with.

'I'm doing okay, Mum. I'm doing more than okay.'

Mum hugged me. 'I'm so proud of you,' she said, and then quickly added, 'Please don't crash.'

I couldn't wait any longer, I sent a text to my friends and included Frankie to try to keep things normal between us. 'Guess who's going to be behind the wheel and driving around town later today? x.'

I included Jane in the message and she replied with a picture of a motorbike helmet saying, 'Your instructor will need one of these, good luck. x.' How rude!

I heard from everyone, except Frankie. Not hearing from her was worse than the awkwardness. It was Sunday morning so she was probably running. I hoped that's what was happening.

Grandpa took my mind off the lack of text reply by taking me out to his car and talking me through the pedals and the controls. I stalled the car as I turned the key, much to his amusement. 'We all have to start somewhere, now, remember what I said about the clutch.'

I hoped I could drive down the road without stalling the instructor's car as I would never live it down otherwise.

Ten

Finally, this morning, I had a reply from Frankie. 'Soz, lots of zzzzzz yesterday & feel crappy x.' She had fallen asleep. She didn't hate me. She had just fallen asleep.

She stayed in bed again today so Sixth Form was quiet without her. I didn't want her to be ill, but having a day where I wasn't constantly worrying about what to say, what not to say, when I saw her, whether I wanted to see her and whether there was a chance I was overthinking all of it, was actually quite nice.

I made it through three lessons and remember some of what was said, which is a miracle.

'Have I just seen you write some notes?' Maya joked, during our first lesson of the day. 'You've put your pen on that piece of paper and written words that are linked to what we're writing our essay on, are you feeling okay?'

'I need to get myself back on track,' I admitted. 'My head's been all over the place and I'm going to fail if I carry on like this.'

As I said the words out loud, I realised that I was genuinely at risk of failing. I was behind on all of my work, hadn't been concentrating, and even though the teachers had been understanding about Grandma and had been patient with me, their patience was understandably wearing thin.

That thought was backed up as I was packing up my bag to go home. 'Nice to have you back in the room, Dani,' my Psychology teacher said.

Has it been that noticeable that my head has been everywhere except where it needs to be? I don't want to be that person. I don't want to fail and I don't want to get myself into the state I've been in before, where there's so much to do and no time to do it.

On top of all the work I'm behind on, I haven't long until my next grading and that's something I really want to pass. I have been trying to follow Lucy's advice and practicing for half an hour or so every day. When I say 'trying', what that really means is I've thought about it and then watched YouTube clips of other people doing their gradings while drinking tea and eating biscuits. I don't think that's what Lucy had in mind when she advised me to 'spend at least thirty minutes a day focusing on your grading'.

I'm being sidetracked by the driving lesson too. That's not a bad thing, I'll enjoy the lessons, but as soon as there's something new and exciting to concentrate on, I forget about everything else. I've even chosen to read the driving theory book rather than practicing for my grading or starting some of the essay I've been trying to ignore. Actually, I've also done some hoovering today rather than working on that essay.

If I can pass my driving test, I can save myself lots of time and drive to places, which means I'll have lots more time to study and practice for my taekwondo gradings. Ah, who am I kidding, I'll just be driving around with my friends and wasting even more time. That's if I'm ever allowed to borrow the car. I think Mum had her eyes closed as she waved me off for that first lesson.

My next driving lesson isn't going to be for a few days and I have another couple of days before I need to totally panic about the essay. I have about three days before I need to panic about all of the other essays, so my aim is to only panic about taekwondo. I just need to stay away from YouTube.

There's a beep from my phone. It's Mum. 'Sorry, hun, I've got to work late as there's a drama here. 'Can you take Reggie and feed yourselves before you go out training? Make sure you eat properly x.'

Mum's given me the perfect excuse to ditch all of my plans to practice before training. I'm not even grumpy about it.

'Walkies? x,' I text Katie. She often comes out with us and

brings her dog, Bailey. He's Reggie's BFF and they have more fun than we do racing around the park and doing their best to check every single tree for squirrels. Bailey is better than Reggie at this. Reggie has been known to just stand at the bottom of the biggest tree, look up and cry while Bailey checks on behalf of them both. They have never caught anything, but that doesn't stop them being just as excited and enthusiastic, every single time. Maybe I should be more like that, not worry so much about the end result but just enjoy the process.

'Yeah, see you in 20, usual place x,' Katie replies. Brilliant, that means Reggie will be extra tired so won't mind when I go training as he can sleep until Mum gets home. It also means an hour of listening to the tales of Cal and whatever he's done lately to annoy Katie, but I don't mind as it means she won't be asking me anything. Once Katie starts on her 'Cal Monologue', there's no stopping her. It's exactly what I need, some company without any pressure and some fresh air.

So, this is another day where I haven't caught up on any of the work I need to do, haven't practiced for my grading and definitely haven't done anything about whether I'm going to apply to go to Uni or not. It's not all bad though because it has been a day where I have managed to listen in lessons, have had a break from my brain permanently thinking about Frankie and have spent some time with my friends. That's slightly more productive than the last few weeks but I have a long way to go if I'm going to leave Sixth Form with decent grades and not have to retake anything.

At the sound of the lead jangling, Reggie is ready. I wish I could be that enthusiastic about the simple things in life.

Eleven

This is silly now. I've spent time tidying up my bedroom, clearing my desk and preparing to work and haven't started actually doing any.

I told my friends yesterday that I'm staying in this weekend because I'm so behind and getting scared.

'You'll spend all weekend doing everything except your assignments and then write a crap one whilst crying on Sunday night,' said the wise, yet annoying Maya. 'You might as well plan to do something fun and then just doing the crying on Sunday night.'

'I won't,' I replied, more to try to convince myself than Maya. 'I'm going to get myself back on track and caught up so that I can try to stop panicking.'

'Good luck,' she scoffed.

It turns out that either Maya knows me better than I thought, or she can see into the future. The only thing she got wrong is that I feel like crying now rather than waiting until tomorrow evening, there's just so much I need to do.

I can't really blame everything that happened over the summer. It's not like I'm a superstar at keeping to deadlines and wouldn't have spent the summer sitting at my desk working hard and loving every minute. I'd have done what I'm doing now on the last day of the holiday. Who knows how I would have been spending the summer if I hadn't raced out of the cinema that night.

Would things be different with Frankie now? I do wish I had stayed until the end of the film, it's not like racing home changed anything. We couldn't have got to Grandma before she died anyway.

Things are kind of back to normal now. Mum still gets upset, but she's fine and helping Grandpa with stuff over the phone. It sounds like Grandma did everything for him. Last night, I was laughing as I could hear Mum's half of the conversation.

'Dad, it's the knob on the left. Turn it to 220 and let the oven heat up before you put your chips in. On the left, left, 220. Go and get your glasses.' She rolled her eyes as I walked past.

I thought about recording the conversations and doing a comedy vlog, until I realised that would keep me occupied for days and probably wasn't the most productive way to spend the weekend. It would be funny, until Mum found out.

Things feel like they're getting back to normal, while not feeling normal at all. Mum's doing okay and Sammy has been great at supporting her. I haven't seen much of him and he was weirdly 'away with work' when Grandpa came to stay so he's smarter than he looks! Being back at Sixth Form and being around the girls is great, although it reminds me of how behind I am. That in itself is quite normal. Katie and Maya are always on top of their work. It comes more naturally to Katie and she seems to get good grades regardless of how much time she spends on an assignment.

Then there's Frankie. It's all okay and we're texting but something is weird. I know it's probably me and I should make a decision, but I don't know what's stopping me. Thinking about it all the time isn't helping as I keep going around in circles.

Do I like her? What am I scared of? Am I feeling this because I'm scared of being with a guy? I've never actually liked a guy, have I? How do I know what's real? Should I tell her the truth about what's going on in my head? Will she think I'm too much hassle and not want to be with me? If we're not together, will she still want to be friends?

The thought of not being friends with Frankie is too much.

Once my head gets full of these questions – it happens about two minutes after I wake up – it's too full to fit anything else in and I'm totally overwhelmed.

'You don't have this problem, do you?' Reggie is lying in the middle of my bedroom, making it as difficult as possible for me to tidy up. He 'helped' by emptying the rubbish bin onto the floor after I had screwed up lots of pieces of paper in order to make my final, colour-coded, to-do list and then bounced around the room with one of those paper balls trying to get me to play, which I did, obviously.

'It sounds like you're going to fall through the ceiling,' Mum had shouted upstairs, which meant 'pack it in, now,' in Mum code. 'I didn't realise you had a dance module to complete.' Another code that had been easy to decipher.

'What would Jane tell me to do?' I ask Reggie. He's drifting off to sleep, which I wish was the answer to my question. 'No, she won't tell me to do that.'

She'll tell me to do my journal stuff, the goals and stuff that she's always banging on about. Then we'll get a plan sorted out so that I can stick to it and make sure I'm able to reach the deadlines, and then she'll say, 'Nobody's going to do this for you, so now you'll just have to follow the plan.'

I don't have time to plan because the deadline for the big assignment is Monday. I just have to get that one done first. I can write my goals though and know that Jane would say that it's a good use of time. So, well done me!

Goals

- It's November and I have my red belt in taekwondo
- It's Monday and I have handed in my essay!

That's enough right now. If I can practice, it'll help clear my head and then I need to just write the freaking essay.

Success

- I haven't cried yet! I know that's not what Jane means about listing things I'm proud of each day, but actually, that's an achievement.

- I haven't crashed during a driving lesson!

Okay, I'll stop with that now. I definitely need to do some things that I can call a success as not crying and not crashing aren't really game-changers.

Gratitude

- I'm grateful that Frankie is still talking to me.
- I'm definitely grateful that I have my best mate with me to help me focus while I work, or just make me laugh when I'm supposed to be working. He's probably the reason I haven't cried about how behind I am, yet!

Now, I need to get a drink and some snacks to help me through the rest of the day.

Twelve

What a full on, crappy week. I've managed to get three assignments done but I'll be lucky if I pass. I apologised as I handed them in. I know that they're rubbish and I'm embarrassed that the teachers will be reading them.

'Done is better than perfect,' Jane has said to me loads of times when I have been stressed out about work. In this case, I think even she would question that philosophy.

I am so tired I want to sleep for a week. It's a good job it's half-term! Sorting myself out is the priority for today. I don't want another week like that – late nights, crying, constant tiredness, feeling grumpy and knowing that I was handing in crap and I could have done loads better if I'd tried.

'Competition for Uni is tough, so you need to be making this year count.' One of my teachers advised as I apologised for what she was about to read. I didn't know whether to be worried that she'd noticed I was doing badly or pleased that she'd thought I could go to Uni.

So, I 'm starting to question whether I'm up to it. If I can't handle Sixth Form, how am I going to handle Uni?

I've got about eight weeks until the end of the year. I know how many assignments I need to do and I know that I might need to plan to re-do some of the ones I've just handed in. I have a couple of exams and I have a lot of revision to do for them. I also want to pass my grading and my driving test.

That's not much, is it? I'm not sure I'll pass my driving test before the end of the year, but I'll need to plan in time for lessons.

How am I going to do all of that in eight weeks? I also want to see my friends and I have to get things sorted properly with Frankie. I have no idea how, but I can't carry on like this. So, by Christmas, things will be sorted, one way or the other.

As I think about it, I know that there is only one option. I just can't figure out how to make that option happen and not totally freak out. Still, that's progress, even if it's only in my head.

I keep thinking out leaving Sixth Form, about going to collect my results and not having a clue what I'm going to do next. At least with the GCSEs, I was pretty sure that I'd get to go to Sixth Form. I didn't admit it at the time, but looking back that was a different sort of pressure to what I'm feeling now. If I don't pass my A Levels, my options don't look great. I also have to figure out where I'm going to live. If I go to Uni away from home, I'll have to move out.

No, no, no. I can't think about that. It's not that I want to stay here, living with Mum forever, but I can't think about leaving. Not right now.

I don't have to decide my whole future today, only what I'm going to do in the next eight weeks. That's fifty-six days. When I put it like that, it sounds like quite a long time.

If I'm going to turn up on results day feeling like I did when I handed my assignments in, that's a total waste of a year. At least with the GCSEs, I felt like I worked hard in the face of the worst year ever and I was happy with the grades. I want to be happy that I've given this my best shot and, at the moment, there's no way I can say that. I'm not doing my best at anything and that's a feeling I don't like at all. I haven't been a good friend, I haven't been fair to Frankie, I haven't been practicing for my grading and Sixth Form is a joke.

I need to sort this out. Eight weeks and then I can enjoy New Year's Eve. Who will I be seeing in the New Year with? That's probably not a question to deal with as a priority.

It's time to make a list, prioritise and then plan what I need to do each week. The dog-training books say that we should set dogs up to succeed and not expect them to learn everything all at once. That keeps coming into my head as there's a cool little table that helps to plan out how to teach a trick. It's in tiny stages. With Reggie at each stage he got a treat so he knew that he was doing well.

'If only getting you to learn something new was that easy,' Mum said as I was teaching Reggie to take a bow. 'You've never been that happy to do your homework.'

'You've never given me treats after each paragraph,' I replied.

I wonder if that will work. If I have a list of the things I love doing, I could have them as a reward for when I've done some work. I definitely don't want the sweaty cheese rewards that Reggie gets so excited about, but I could definitely work for Maltesers. One paragraph = one Malteser. That's got to be worth a try.

Thirteen

I tried so hard to make Operation Malteser Reward work for me. It was going well until I became stuck on a question, started to research the answer and finished off the entire box without even thinking about it. It was like my hand was working independently to my body and feeding my face while my eyes were frantically searching for an answer that made sense.

'You've finished your essay then?' Mum said as she brought me a drink.

'Not exactly, I might need to rethink the reward system,' I admitted, and felt the need to add, 'I actually feel a bit sick.'

'I'll take the box away and you can reward yourself with a salad when you finish that one.'

'Yum.' A salad didn't sound too bad in all honesty. Not necessarily as a reward but even I couldn't face the thought of eating anything else sweet.

'Remember that we have to be ready to leave to see Amie soon, so get writing, come down for lunch in an hour or so and we'll head off.'

As soon as I had a deadline of an hour, I felt like I had been turbocharged into getting the essay finished. It was weird, but when I had loads of time, I didn't get much done, but once the time was limited, I was on a mission. My fingers were racing over the keys, I had more ideas than I knew what to do with, and when I read through it, I was quite proud of myself. It made sense, it answered the question and it had a decent conclusion. Maybe having a time limit needed to feature in my plans to get back on track, as that had worked better than stuffing my face with chocolate.

Because I ticked off one of my major headaches on my to-do list, I enjoyed spending time with Amie and her mum. I can't say I enjoyed the salad very much, but it balanced out the box of

Maltesers and made me feel slightly less guilty about the amount of crap I'd eaten.

Seeing Amie always left me with mixed feelings. We were only friends because we had the monumentally shitty shared experience of being rape survivors. If it wasn't for that, we'd never have met. Our Mums had become really close friends and I guessed Amie and I were close, but there was an age gap of a couple of years which meant I sometimes found her quite annoying. Being older, I felt like I should be the one that was helping her and offering her words of wisdom. It had started out that way when we had first met, as it had been so soon after she had been attacked. I had been the person who had genuinely been able to say that things would get better. She hadn't believed me at the time, but that had been fair enough, I hadn't believed anyone when they'd said that to me in the early days either. We had both felt that nothing would ever be okay again, ever. We were both wrong and on days like today, we proved to ourselves and to each other that life didn't just become bearable, but could actually be pretty awesome.

We hadn't seen each other since early on in the summer holidays because of all the stuff that had been going on with Grandma and being busy at weekends. Well, supposedly being busy, but it was mainly just procrastinating and crying over my hundredth to-do list without actually ticking anything off it.

Amie was doing well and, as usual, she inspired me. For someone who struggled so much in those early days, understandably so, she had totally turned things around. She bragged about getting so many As that she'd lost count, and she also told me she was on the student mentoring programme where she was helping the younger kids in school.

'I bet you're awesome at that,' I said, honestly. 'I could have done with a mentor like you when I was at school.'

'Yeah, I'm all right I suppose, and I do love it.'

'It's okay to say that you're good at something, Amie,' I told her, immediately feeling like a fraud.

'Okay, I'm freaking awesome at mentoring and I'm totally helping those kids change their lives.'

'WOW, you're buzzing about this. What are you doing with them?' As Amie came to life explaining about the kids, I felt a bit emotional. It was obvious that being a mentor wasn't just helping change the lives of the younger kids, but it was changing Amie's too.

'One lad, Ayo, told me that his name means "full of joy" and he literally is. He's the happiest kid I've ever met.'

'Why does he need a mentor then?' I asked, thinking that these programmes were usually for the kids who needed extra support, or kids who were getting themselves into lots of trouble.

'His mum and brother died back in the country he was born in and now he lives here with his dad and his other two brothers. One of his brothers is in the same year as me. He's a mentor too and seriously good-looking.'

'Two members of his family died and he's the happiest kid you've ever met?' I was confused and wanted to know his secret. 'How has he recovered from that?'

'He said that he misses them every day, but his dad talks about how grateful they should all be to have known them, that his mum gave him life and that his brother is looking out for them all as their own personal angel. He said he can't waste a second on this earth and that he says "thank you and I love you" to his mum every day.'

I could feel my eyes were about to leak tears. 'What an incredible family,' I said, thinking that I couldn't remember the last time I had said 'thank you and I love you' to my own mum.

'They really are. I know that we've had a rough time and have a lot to figure out in our heads, but we can't even begin to imagine what they've seen and experienced. I'm so happy that they're here now, where they're safe and they're totally going to change the world. They're all really smart and so lovely and

I wish their dad would marry my mum so he could be my dad too.'

'Does your mum know about that plan?' I laughed, wondering if Amie would deal with that a lot better than I did when Mum first met Sammy.

'Nah, they haven't met, but I reckon I could figure something out.'

By the sound of it, Amie was already plotting. It was only on the way home that I realised it was one of the first times we'd been out and just talked and had a laugh. It wasn't about how we were doing, how we were coping or who'd had a rough time recently. We had been just two people, catching up and talking about what was going on in our lives.

We really were doing more than okay and it felt good.

Fourteen

Today has been full on work, work, work so that tomorrow I can spend the day with Frankie. It's back to Sixth Form next week and I'm determined by then to have caught up, to hand in the essays and to feel like I've done a good job.

So far, the new plan is working and I've stuck to it. First, I sorted everything in the diary carefully. I planned for Reggie's walks, my lunch breaks, which essays I needed to do and in which order, when I had to do research for them, and I even added in 20-minute bursts of taekwondo practice throughout each day (which is helping my brain more than my body I think).

'I'm proud of you,' Mum told me last night. 'You seem to have turned a corner with Sixth Form, which I must admit is a relief.'

It was nice that she had noticed. I thought I'd been able to hide how far behind I was, but obviously not.

'If there's anything I can do to help, just let me know. Is there anything you need? I can take Reggie out before and after work if you need more study time.'

'No way, but thanks. That's part of the plan to keep me sane. Going out with him wakes me up in the morning and then gives me something to look forward to after a day of mind numbingly boring essays.'

'Aren't you enjoying it at all?' She seemed concerned.

Like who actually enjoys writing essays? 'I like it when I've finished?' I offered, which was enough to make her relax and leave me to it. Working to the soundtrack of Reggie snoring was funny. I was half-jealous that he could just stretch out anywhere and sleep so soundly, and half-pleased that he was with me but not being annoying.

I was trying to finish an essay a couple of days ago, and right when I was in my flow, he came thundering up the stairs with his favourite squeaky toy, dropped it at my feet and then spun around, his tail obliterating my tea and the biscuits Mum had left for me. He hoovered up the biscuits and ran off again, leaving me to tidy up and by the time I sat back down to carry on, I had forgotten my genius sentence.

It's a good job he's cute.

Getting on with all of this work has helped me to think about Frankie only ninety-five per cent of the time and not one hundred per cent of the time. That is progress. We're messaging a lot, but haven't been able to see each other very often, so we've decided that we should have a day to hang out before we go back to Sixth Form.

We're both supposed to have caught up on our work so that we can enjoy tomorrow, but I think I'm the only one working.

'Wish u woz here x,' came the first message this morning. Frankie had gone for a long run and sent me a picture of her blowing a kiss. She was on top of hill, and I didn't recognise where it was so who knew how far she'd run.

'That's some impressive avoidance tactics x,' I replied, wondering if I'd ever get to a point where I thought running was a better option than writing essays. I doubted it very much.

I love hearing from Frankie and I love that she messages me, I even get a weird but kind of nice feeling in my stomach when I see her name pop up, but sometimes I wish she'd just take the piss out of me, like she used to. She's much more flirty now and I guess I feel a bit awkward because we don't know for sure what's going on between us.

I miss having my friend. The friend I could message about how crap it was to have so much work to do, the friend who would slag off the creepy guy at the coffee shop because he kept staring at us, and the friend who understood me and accepted me without question.

Now, she is more likely to send me a message like that, with her blowing a kiss, than one whinging about work or just a message that says she's going running because she's avoiding writing her essay.

I guess, more than anything, I want my friend back. Would that be enough? Would that be the best option for all of us?

Focus, Dani. Focus. I have to finish these essays before tomorrow so I can actually enjoy myself and see what happens.

Having this new plan in my life definitely helps with the daydreaming about Frankie because I have to finish something before I get to go out with Reggie. That's next on the list and luckily, he's still snoring his head off so won't mind waiting another half an hour.

Fifteen

Today was supposed to be fun. I thought we could hang out, have a laugh and remember what it was like before there was all this pressure.

Frankie had a different idea about why we were meeting up. She thought we were going to be talking about us – what was going on and what was going to happen next.

'I can't deal with being in limbo all the time. One minute I think we might be giving it a go and the next minute you're blanking me. I just want to know where I stand.'

That was Frankie's way of saying 'hello' and it left me feeling quite shell-shocked.

'Can't we just hang out and have a laugh' I said, desperately trying to lighten the mood and in the hope that I could change the subject. 'Did you get that essay done in the end?'

'Jesus, Dani! Who cares about the essay?' I thought she might storm off, so I carried on talking in the hope she'd chill out a bit.

'Erm, me! I don't want to get thrown out of Sixth Form, because then I'd only get to see you when you're in town and grumpy.'

She actually smiled. I think she heard my sigh of relief and I thought we might be able to have a good day after all.

'You do want to see me then?'

'Of course.' Had I not made that obvious? I was right there, sitting in front of her. Why would I choose to spend the day with her if I didn't want to see her?

'I don't get it. We said we liked each other. I know that you've had a lot going on and I've tried to be patient, but weeks are going by and nothing's changing. You said you wanted to meet up today and I really thought you'd be putting me out of my misery.'

'Misery?' That word was a kick in the gut. 'Am I making you

miserable?'

'You know what I mean. I don't know what's going on and I can't think about anything else. At least if I knew one way or the other, I could then stop worrying about it all the time.'

'I never wanted to make you miserable.' I was gutted. I had been so caught up in how I was feeling that I hadn't thought about the impact it was having on Frankie. While I was finding it annoying that she was sending me those messages, she was trying to figure out what was going on. Did she really like me that much? I looked at her and she wouldn't look back at me. She was playing with her headphones, staring down while she twisted them around her fingers. I'd only ever seen her doing that when she knew she was about to get told her essay was late and she was worried about what was going to happen. I didn't know what to say to make things better. I knew what Frankie wanted me to say. I wanted to say those words but I couldn't. I just couldn't.

'I miss us being friends,' I whispered. I didn't mean it to sound like that was all I wanted, but that was what came out of my mouth. I meant that we'd had so much fun when we were friends. We'd talked, we'd laughed, the time had flown by and I'd always walked away from Frankie already looking forward to the next time I'd see her. Right now, neither of us were having a good time, we were both hurting and unhappy and surely that wasn't right? If you liked someone, that was supposed to be a good thing, wasn't it? I never thought it could feel like this.

'I can't do this, Dani. I don't want to just be friends.' With that, Frankie stood up, put her headphones on and walked away.

'Now what?' I said to myself. My eyes filled with tears. *'Had I just lost the best thing that never happened to me?'* I watched her walk away and I pleaded with my legs to get up and follow her, to chase her and tell her exactly how I felt. I wanted to tell her the truth, tell her how frightened I was that I couldn't trust my feelings and tell her that the last thing I ever wanted to do was

hurt her.

Instead, my eyes leaked tears into my hot chocolate as I stared at my phone, willing it to beep and for a message from Frankie to appear. It didn't happen.

I had done the very thing that I didn't want to do. I had hurt Frankie and I had no idea what to do about it.

Walking around the shops by myself was no fun at all. I saw groups of friends laughing together, couples walking hand in hand and suddenly a wave of loneliness washed over me. I hadn't felt anything like it for a long time. It was a harsh reminder of how good things had been and how it could all change in a heartbeat. I walked home, still hoping that I'd hear from Frankie.

As I threw myself onto my bed and crawled under the duvet, I realised that she might be doing exactly the same thing. Was she staring at her phone hoping to hear from me or had I totally screwed up and she was hoping never to hear from me again?

It had been a long time since I had crawled under the duvet, wanting the escape from the world. It wasn't a good feeling at all.

I cried. I cried until I could hardly breathe and I hadn't even noticed that Reggie had followed me upstairs. He was sitting by my bed, his head resting on the mattress. By his feet was his favourite toy, which he looked at, picked up in his mouth and dropped by my pillow. He wasn't bouncing around trying to play, he was trying to help, trying to make me smile. At least I could trust my feelings when it came to Reggie. I loved him unconditionally, and the feeling was mutual.

If I could trust myself so completely about this matter, then what was so different about another human being, who also liked me. Maybe not unconditionally, but she said she liked me. What was so different?

Sixteen

'Keep avoiding it, Dani, and it'll never go away. x,' came the annoyingly perceptive message from Jane.

Mum must have told her that I was missing Sixth Form today and that I didn't look ill at all. There's a reason why I didn't take drama. My acting skills leave a lot to be desired. Back in my old school, my old life, or what has become known as 'before', my drama teacher actually wrote in my report: 'Dani tries hard in class but I feel her talents lie in the production of performances, not on stage.'

I remember Mum trying to hold back her laughter as she said that there was a lot of money to be made in production. 'You know, behind the scenes, Dani, that's where the fun really is.'

Yeah, that had been a really good way of boosting my confidence after being told I was rubbish at acting. Luckily, I had never fancied life as an actress and it meant that Mum was even more supportive of me doing PE, which I was actually okay at.

Anyway, I told Mum that I wasn't feeling well this morning. I even held my stomach and used my most pathetic 'but I'm poorly' voice.

'One day, Dani. One day and then you get yourself back to Sixth Form.'

I didn't push my luck and nodded. She left for work.

The really annoying thing was that I wanted to go to Sixth Form today, I had finished my assignment and was okay with what I'd done. Emailing it in didn't have quite the same feeling of satisfaction as actually handing it over. Not just handing it over, but handing it over on time. I was only avoiding Frankie. I couldn't face her. Not yet. Not today.

I haven't heard from her since she walked away from me and I haven't messaged her either. I don't know what to say. I've started about 400 messages and deleted them because I can't bring myself to press send.

Even though I know it doesn't work, I have a habit of avoiding things I am uncomfortable about. Not only does it not work, it usually makes me feel worse and makes the whole situation worse. Right now, I'm hurting myself, I'm hurting Frankie and I'm missing Sixth Form. That is stupid. I know it's stupid and yet I'm still sitting here, not doing anything about it.

Jane's right. Of course, she's right. By sitting here driving myself insane I'm making everything worse. The situation isn't going away and I'm not even hiding from it as it's with me all the time. I can't stop thinking about it all.

Right, today has to count for something and I refuse to sabotage everything just because I'm taking the easy way out. Well, it doesn't feel easy, but at least I don't have to face Frankie and try to get through a lesson with her. That's too much to deal with while things are so weird between us.

I can take Reggie out, as long as I'm not spotted. Mum took him out before she left for work so we can wait until later and if anyone sees me I'll just say I'm feeling a bit better. I can do some practice for my grading, which I definitely need to do. That'll focus my brain as it takes so much concentration. I can't wait for the day it comes naturally to me, like it does for Lucy. Watching her going through all the moves was incredible. I bet she doesn't avoid training.

I could also do some work. Weird, I suddenly feel genuinely poorly! What is worse, going into Sixth Form and facing Frankie, or getting some work done at home, while wearing my pyjamas and curling up on the sofa with Reggie? Hmmm, that's a tough one. Maybe getting some work done isn't such a bad idea after all. I have my plan all sorted and all I have to do is stick to it. I've already messed up by not going to classes today, but that doesn't mean I totally have to waste the day.

I know what Jane would tell me to do, so I'll actually take her advice and try to get focused.

Goals

- It's November and I have my red belt in taekwondo
- Mum's home from work tonight and I have finished an essay.
- It's the end of December and I have stuck to my plan.

Success

- Hmmm, I definitely don't feel like I have succeeded in anything over the last few days. I did send one essay in this morning, so that's got to count. Other than not actually going into Sixth Form today, which we won't dwell on, I've caught up with the work I was behind on and now just need to stay on top of all the other deadlines. So, it's not all bad.

Gratitude

- I'm grateful that I can be at home, that Mum didn't give me loads of grief for skiving off and that I can hide away while I try to figure out what to do next.

Reaching for my phone, I'm pleased to see that Katie has messaged me. She must be worried that she hasn't seen me.

'Have you & Frankie eloped? x,' reads the message.

'What? x,' I manage to reply. Eloped? What does she mean by that? Has Frankie said something to her? She wouldn't, would she?

'Where are you both? x.'

Both? Does that mean Frankie hasn't turned up either? Are you freaking kidding me? I'm avoiding her and she's obviously avoiding me too. This is just stupid.

'I'm ill, will see u tomo x,' I reply, resisting the urge to ask Katie if she has heard from Frankie. She will think it's weird that

I don't know where she is.

'Yeah, yeah, course you are x,' is her fair, but annoying reply.

This is enough to send my mind spinning again.

Seventeen

The answer came to me earlier in the middle of my grading.

Back home I ponder on it all. Overall, it's a pretty amazing way to start a new month; with a new belt. It's my red belt and while that feels really good, there's something missing – I usually text my friends to tell them and wait for the sarcastic responses about coloured pyjamas and not messing with me anymore. This time, I haven't told anyone.

Things with Frankie have almost been too much for me to deal with. I've avoided seeing her as much as possible and when I have seen her, it's been way too awkward. She has made it clear that I have to tell her what I want, one way or the other. She has also been more than clear about what she wants.

I've dealt with this like a proper grown up and avoided her, ploughing all of my energy into my grading and even reaching the depths of despair recently when I chose to write one of my essays before the deadline. That was the point when I realised I was taking my avoidance to a whole new level. It could be worse, a couple of years ago, I would have hidden under the duvet with boxes of Jaffa Cakes and distracted myself with YouTube videos of cute kittens and puppies. I've only done that once in the last couple of weeks. Okay, twice. Only twice though, so that's pretty impressive by my standards.

'I know something's up, Dani,' Mum said earlier. 'When I brought you a snack, it looked like you were actually studying.' Mum laughed and tried to start a conversation.

'You have a go at me when I am behind with work and you take the piss when I'm trying to get stuff done, I can't do anything right,' I snapped back, immediately regretting it.

That wasn't fair, but it wasn't like I could tell her what was actually wrong. She would never understand. Nobody would understand.

I went over and over it in my head. What was the worst thing that could happen? It felt like that worst thing had already happened, I felt like I'd lost Frankie. It was not just that I'd lost my friend, it was that I still felt a wave of excitement in my stomach when I saw her. Nobody seemed to have told my stomach that we were not really talking. I read, and re-read, old messages. They were different to the messages I sent to the others. I found some selfies we took on our last day out with Reggie. We were close in those pictures. Physically close. My stomach did that thing again when I looked at them. Why was I being such an idiot? I had someone who actually liked me. I just didn't believe she would still like me if she knew what a total mess I was. She brought out the best me, but she hadn't seen me at my worst. Why would anyone want to be with me when I was scared of getting close to them?

There were still tears in my eyes as I got ready for my grading. I couldn't eat, which was always a sign that something wasn't right. Reggie laid his head on my lap as I sat and watched the ticking clock. I was early. What was wrong with me?

'Is that good luck dribble?' I asked him. I could feel my knee was a little bit soggy and hoped that it would be dry by the time I stood up and took my position for the grading. 'It wouldn't be the same without some good luck dribble.' He pottered off to his bed; happy with his perfectly executed 'good luck' message.

A few minutes later I set off and walked to the building that had become a second home to me. It was my safe place. I loved going in, seeing the same faces and feeling like I belonged. It was mine. It was something totally separate to Sixth Form, to family, to friends and something that didn't have any links to Frankie. It was just mine. At least, I liked to think it was.

As I approached the main hall, Mum suddenly appeared through the door. 'Like I'd miss this, good luck, baby girl,' she said.

'How did you know?'

'You should know by now, I don't miss a thing.'

That was quite a scary thought. If she didn't miss a thing, then what else did she know about? Frankie popped in to my head again and I forced myself to shut her out. 'This is my time, this is my time, this is my time,' I repeated over and over again in my head. In that moment, all I wanted was to pass my grading. In that moment, nothing else mattered.

All of the practice turned out to be worth it. I might not have always been doing it for the right reasons, but then I never thought there would ever be a wrong reason to practice something you loved, something that was good for you and something that made you feel proud of yourself. I was proud of myself. I passed my grading.

As had become tradition, we drove home via the takeaway. It was actually a complete detour, and not on the way home at all, but it was always a welcome drive.

'That was amazing,' Mum proudly declared. 'I've sat through a lot of gradings, but that one was something special. You looked like a pro.'

Okay, so that was going a bit far, but I was pleased she could see that I had improved. 'Thanks, I did okay.'

'Only okay? Well, if that's "okay", I can't wait to see what you do when you're "pretty good" and getting the next belt. But first, we're celebrating this one.'

I had something else to celebrate. In the middle of my grading, the answer had come to me. I didn't want to lose Frankie, but I also didn't want her to like only the version of me she had seen so far. I wanted her to know why I was afraid, why I couldn't leap into a relationship with her. I desperately wanted her to know that I was sorry for hurting her and that it was nothing to do with how awesome she was. She needed to know that I thought she was awesome.

So sitting here in my room now, I think more about it. What's the worst that can happen if I just tell her the truth? That was what came to me in that burst of inspiration. It's my biggest fear and the only solution, all rolled into one. The worst thing that can happen is that she decides she doesn't want to be with me, or be friends with me after all. If that happens, then I know that she's not the person I want to be with anyway. Even worse than that, she might walk away and then tell other people, but I've dealt with worse. Then, there's the other question. What's the best thing that could happen? When I start to think about that, the wave of excitement in my stomach goes into overdrive.

Eighteen

So, telling the truth turned out not to be the worst thing in the world after all.

I thought it would be. I thought that telling Frankie the whole truth would be the start of another nightmare, that it would mean losing her for good and destroying the best thing that had ever happened to me. What she said though tore me apart and comforted me all at the same time.

'I think you might have underestimated me a little bit,' she whispered, and held my hand.

I had sent her a message while I was enjoying my celebratory takeaway. 'Hey, fancy meeting up tomo, for lunch, my treat x.'

Actually, it was Mum's treat as she had given me some money to do something fun and celebrate my red belt. I couldn't think of anything I wanted to do more than see Frankie.

'Sure, I'd luv to x,' she replied. That felt good. She still wanted to see me and that had to be a good sign. I hadn't totally ruined it then.

My stomach was in knots as I waited for her outside our favourite café. As soon as I got there, I knew I had made a mistake. Not about seeing her or about telling her the truth, but there was no way I was going to sit in a busy café and talk about stuff. We'd spent a lot of time in the same café laughing about the conversations we could overhear. I should have thought that through. I needed a Plan B.

'Fancy going for a walk first? It's really busy in there,' I said as soon as Frankie arrived.

'A walk? Without Reggie? How weird.' She smiled and we headed off in the direction of the park.

'You could have picked a warmer day for a trek.'

That was a fair comment. I was still plucking up the courage to start telling Frankie all of the things I was so desperate to tell her. After hours of worrying about it, I hadn't actually figured out how I was going to start the conversation.

'Let's sit down.'

'Yeah, that's a great idea, Dani, let's get even colder,' she joked as she sat on the bench and wrapped her jacket tightly around her.

Once I started, I couldn't stop. Frankie sat with me, giving me her undivided attention and she didn't say a word. I started with how happy I had been in my old school, how I didn't realise how good life was back then. I told her that I had been raped on my way home from school and that after the court case was over, we had moved here. I apologised for telling her that we'd moved for Mum's job, but that's what we told everyone and it had almost become the truth for us. I told her about Reggie, my life-changing best friend. I didn't even feel silly when I admitted that without him, I was not sure I'd still be here. That boy saved my life, little by little, day by day, and had made the world a safe place for me again. More than that, he'd made the world a fun place to be. I told her about the bullies, in more detail than maybe I should have done, especially as a couple of them went to her running club. Then I told her about how life had become great again. Starting Sixth Form, meeting her. Mainly just meeting her.

'You see, I'm not trying to hurt you. The last thing on earth I want to do is mess you around. I just want to be sure that what I'm feeling is real. I do like you. I really do like you, a lot. I'm just scared, I guess. I'm scared that telling you all this will put you off me, but not telling you feels wrong too.'

I ran out of words. I felt exhausted and terrified that it was all going to be for nothing. I'd just taken the biggest risk of my life.

When Frankie whispered those words, I knew the risk had been worth it.

'Nothing you've told me changes how I feel. If anything, it's made me like you more and I didn't think that was possible.

You're the strongest person I've ever met and I'm honoured that you've trusted me with this. I promise you I won't tell a soul, you can trust me.'

The relief made me cry.

'Jeez, you can say all that and only now your eyes are watering,' she said. 'I'm here, I'm not going anywhere and you can take all the time you need. Just don't go quiet on me again.'

'I won't,' I promised, and I meant it. I wasn't going to risk losing her, not again. 'Lunch?

'I seriously thought you'd never ask.'

Eating lunch with Frankie was paradise. We laughed and joked like we used to. I was worried that even if things went well, she might treat me differently, might not know what to say, or would ask me loads of questions.

She was right, I had totally underestimated her.

Nineteen

The last couple of weeks have been a blur. I have been floating around in a bubble of happiness, something I never thought I'd experience and honestly never realised existed. Frankie has stuck to her word and hasn't put any pressure on me at all. I have my friend back; better than that, all the awkwardness has gone and when she holds my hand, I feel like the luckiest girl alive. This hasn't helped my concentration levels and I'm behind on my work, but I'm not sure I care. I'm supposed to be making the most of today as a study day while Frankie is away at a running training thing, but I miss her and can't wait to see her.

Feeling like this got me thinking about Mum too. I can't even begin to imagine how she must have felt when the sperm donor, or 'Dad' I suppose I should call him, abandoned her and simply never reappeared. How did she deal with that? She had me to deal with too. I was a baby, so arguably more hassle than I am now, although Mum might not agree. As Grandpa said, 'You were cuter then, but we couldn't leave you at home all day like we can now.'

I know that she loves Sammy and considering how well I took that when she told me, that can't have been easy for her either. Wow, she really has put up with a lot from me! I wonder what she'll say when I tell her about Frankie? I hope she deals with it better than I dealt with her and Sammy. I definitely won't be able deal with tantrums! I'd have to send her to Jane's, although she'd love that!

'It's nice to see that you've cheered up,' was all she said after I came back from talking to Frankie. Other than that, she hasn't made any comments and she's probably enjoying some peace. I've definitely cheered up, that's for sure.

I know it's only been a couple of weeks, but trusting Frankie was definitely a good decision. So far, anyway.

'You know I'm always here if you want to talk,' was the only reference she made to our conversation and that was perfect. Any fear I had of it being weird or her not knowing what to say disappeared. She knew exactly what to say. She's now gone back to taking the piss, to making me laugh and to being the Frankie I knew before it got weird.

I know that it was a risk to trust her. It was a risk to trust anyone. This time, it has worked out brilliantly and I believe her when she says that she won't tell anyone. I hope she has forgiven me for being so distant and that she understands now. Her actions are telling me everything I need to know. She's amazing.

I wasn't sure if I'd ever be able to trust anyone like this. I wasn't sure if I'd ever *want* to trust anyone like this. There's a fine line between wanting to explain why something is difficult and making an excuse not to. The fears around being judged, or being seen differently, are huge, and you never really know until you take the risk.

I remember the first time we went to the rescue centre to look for our new family member. Mum wanted a small dog that was easy to manage and we ended up with a seven stone plonker who chose us. There was something about me that enabled him to trust me. I don't know what it was but I'm forever grateful it happened. Mum didn't even want to meet him to start with as she said there was no way we could cope with a dog that size. I knew the thought of his food bill also worried her. It still does! Reggie had been rescued from a mother and daughter who had hurt him in ways that I would never be able to deal with. Yet, there he was, with a mother and daughter combination, putting his trust in us almost instantly.

How did he know? How did he allow himself to trust us?

Reggie and I have a lot in common, we've both had stuff happen to us and we've both had to figure out how to come out the other side of it.

I think of Reggie's time in the rescue kennels as similar to my time going through court. We were safe, but still in the nightmare.

When we collected Reggie to bring him home, and when the sentence was handed down to 'him', we were able start again. We both had a fresh start.

Reggie coped with his fresh start much better than I coped with mine. It's taken me longer to learn to trust my instinct again. He came home and after some excitement that was encouraged by me, he slept by my side for hours. It was a deep sleep, something he hadn't been able to do at the rescue centre with the noise and the uncertainty. He lay next to me, trusting me. He felt safe enough to sleep and that was something I still never take for granted. I know that being able to sleep peacefully is pure magic.

I have slept again since trusting Frankie, and that says a lot. I don't know if I'll ever learn to trust in the way Reggie does, so completely and unconditionally, but I want to try. He has overcome the crap times and allowed himself to trust us, so I can follow his example and do the same.

The only small challenge with him being a happy, sleepy dog is that I now have to try to write these assignments to the soundtrack of him snoring. It's annoying, and weirdly relaxing at the same time. I wouldn't have it any other way though. Having him lying here while I work is the best company I could ask for.

Twenty

A couple of weeks into December Mum decided we needed to put up the decorations.

'Isn't it a bit early for all this?' I pleaded as Mum started to climb the ladder to the loft.

'I want everything looking nice for when your grandpa's here next weekend and I won't have time to do it in the evenings.' Mum was getting grumpy already and she hadn't passed the first box down yet.

'But he said not to make a fuss.' They were his exact words when he said he'd come and see us before Christmas but was going to spend the day itself with one of his friends who had also lost his wife this year. How sad was that? At least they would have some company, but we were all pretty sure they'd have beans on toast as neither of them could cook.

'Are you going to help me or not?'

That wasn't actually a question. It was Mum's way of saying, 'Shut up, we're doing this and you will help me.' Why couldn't she just have said that?

Having boxes of decorations dropped on me from a great height wasn't my idea of a fun way to spend a morning, but watching Reggie racing around the house with tinsel and baubles was always entertaining.

'At least someone is looking forward to Christmas,' Mum said, more to herself than to me so I ignored it.

She made some comments about it being her first Christmas without her mum and how it was a difficult time of the year when you were grieving. I got that and I got it was hard to see all those annoying adverts with happy families that had been out since October and the cards with 'Mum' written on them. What I didn't get was that over the last couple of years, well, longer than that to be honest, my mum had dreaded a visit from her mum and had spent most of December figuring out ways to avoid seeing her. She didn't have to see her at all now, so I wasn't sure why she was making such a big deal out of it.

Making the house 'look nice' was another matter. As soon as we got something up on the tree and Mum had moved it two hundred times until it was 'just right', Reggie decided it looked much better in his mouth and added to his extensive collection of soggy Christmas decorations that were being stored on his bed. Apparently, this was not funny.

'You're encouraging him to do that,' Mum shouted as she shut the living room door, with Reggie on the other side of it.

'He's having fun' I argued. 'Isn't this supposed to be fun?'

'You're right,' were words I don't think I have ever heard Mum say to me before. She sank into the sofa, looking tired and fed up. 'This is supposed to be fun, and it doesn't feel like fun at all.'

'Let's forget about it and do it later,' I offered as a solution, hoping that would get me out of being there at all.

'Nice try.' Nope, that wasn't going to work. 'Let's get some music on and try and get into the festive spirit.'

'Magical,' I managed. Crap Christmas songs were all we needed to make the day go from bad to worse. Or so I thought.

The tears came as Mum whispered, 'Your grandma loved this song.'

'Did she?' I wasn't convinced and I couldn't remember Grandma ever getting excited about any Christmas songs. Grandpa would attempt to sing-a-long to some of them, which was painful for all of us, but not Grandma. She was the first to tell him to 'put a sock in it'. 'I know she liked this,' I reminisced, finding one of the disgusting decorations I had made at primary school.

'Nobody likes that, Dani. We were just trying to be nice.'

'Can you remember what it was supposed to be?'

'Absolutely no idea,' Mum admitted, pulling out all the

decorations I had created over the years.

'Maybe we should let Reggie destroy these instead of the good ones,' I suggested, opening the door to let him back in.

'See, even Reggie thinks they're rubbish.' She laughed and Reggie curled up on the sofa, not taking the risk that he might get evicted again. 'I bet he'll miss your grandma this year too, she loved to give him some of her food when we weren't looking.'

'Mum, she didn't. She told us she didn't want him near the table and occasionally threw a bit of meat as far as she could to send him away.'

'Ah, she loved him really.'

'Yes, she did and I'm not saying she didn't, but I don't get why you're making such a big deal out of this. You didn't like it when she visited and she got on your nerves for most of the time she was here.'

Okay, that might have been a bit harsh as Mum looked shocked and upset by my mini-outburst rather than her usual 'angry' look.

'Dani, your grandma and I had a difficult relationship. She said some things that hurt me, that really hurt me, but it doesn't take away the fact that she also made me who I am today. She taught me to stand up for what I believe in, she taught me to fight for what I want and she stood by me when I was left alone with you and I was absolutely terrified.'

I didn't have much to say in response to that, but Mum wasn't done yet.

'I wish things had been different over the last few years. When you were attacked, I didn't only feel that I'd let you down. I felt that I'd let them down. It was, and still is, my job to keep you safe. They loved you from before you were born and the first time your grandma held you, she looked at me and said, "You're going to be brilliant at being this little one's mum. Keep her safe for us." I wish I'd had the courage to talk to her before she died. I wish I could tell her that I did my best and I will always do my best, just as she did for me.'

I really didn't have a clue, did I? While I was doing okay and feeling proud of myself for being more than okay, I forgot that what happened had such a huge impact on everyone else too.

'Sorry,' I said.

Twenty-One

Christmas is a time when there isn't much time to do a lot of work because of all that's going on. It's made me panic. Worrying about Mum hasn't helped.

'Wow, that got really heavy,' Frankie said when I told her about Mum's little outburst. 'It's kind of sad though, you know, that she feels she didn't say all of the things she wanted to say.'

'It is, but I hope she chills out about it all before Grandpa turns up. He's having a tough time and the last thing he needs is Mum talking about how Grandma loved the sprouts, or the tinsel or the bloody wrapping paper.'

'You're going to have so much fun at your first Christmas weekend, aren't you?' she joked. Frankie was jealous that I was going to have two Christmas dinners, but now she could see that it wasn't going to be as much fun as it might have sounded. 'So, I've been thinking,' she added.

'I thought I could smell burning,' I quipped.

'Funny. I was thinking that because you were already having two Christmases, you might want to go for a full set and have a third one with me?'

'I'm not cooking, unless you want pizza.' I had told Frankie that my cooking skills were non-existent a while ago and then had quickly changed the subject when she'd made a joke about needing to be a better housewife. My brain hadn't been ready to hear the word 'housewife', not even as a joke.

'Seriously, it would be fun. My folks are going away so we could swap presents, have a Christmas dinner of pizza, if that's what you want, and then watch Christmas films.'

I think she could sense the mild panic rising as soon as she mentioned that her folks wouldn't be home.

'Bring Reggie, there's no pressure, I just thought it would be a laugh.'

I could definitely cope with pizza, films and a laugh. 'Sounds perfect, I'll even splash out on some mince pies, if you're not sick of them by then.'

'Never,' said the mince pie addict. 'So, that's settled, we'll have Christmas our way. We can take Reggie to the pub for lunch if it's not too cold to sit outside, and then have pizza for dinner.'

It did sound like fun and once I'd got over the initial panic, I was excited at the thought of our own Christmas. I was sure that Mum wouldn't mind, especially as I was taking Reggie. She complained a lot about walking him in the cold weather so it would be a bonus for her. I didn't have a clue what to get Frankie. It needed to be a special present without being too full-on. How would I manage that?

Thinking about it now, I'm pretty sure that Frankie would rather I didn't bring Reggie with me. She knows that he's like a giant security blanket for me though, so it's nice of her. The second she said I could, I felt much more relaxed. The fact she was more interested in planning her meals than anything else made me laugh too. That's definitely the Frankie I know, with her priority always being food. That's probably why she would prefer it if Reggie stayed at home, I'll give him my leftovers and not her!

So, the only problem with having all of these Christmases is I have no idea when I'm going to get my work done. We have Grandpa coming, then Jane and Lucy are coming for a long weekend and then I'll be at Frankie's before term starts. My plan was going so well over the last couple of weeks and I've ditched it in favour of seeing Frankie. I can't say that's a bad thing as I've been having a really good time, but it's hardly going to make me a success.

Last week, we got our results back for a test we'd done in PE. Somehow, Frankie managed to get an 'A' and I only got a 'C'.

'Being happy is working out well for me,' she joked, until she saw my face and then my grade. 'Oh, not working out so well for you.'

No, it isn't working out so well for me at all. I wouldn't change it and I definitely wouldn't go back to when it was awkward and horrible, but I would like to go back to getting good grades. The panic of potentially failing is bubbling away again.

Goals

I have to get my head around these again. I seem to spend more time planning that I do actually getting stuff done. If I'd just stuck to the plan, I'd be flying.

- It is May and I have my black tag. That's the last step before I can think about my black belt. It's in reach; my dream of being a black belt isn't that far away now. It's going to take about six months to get to the stage where I can think about the grading, but only if I work hard or it'll be longer. That's also around the time I'll be leaving Sixth Form, so I need to have a focus that isn't the exams or I'll lose the plot.
- It's New Year and I have spent time with my friends. I desperately don't want to be the sort of person that Katie was when she started seeing Cal. She was so annoying, never had time for her friends and talked about him non-stop. I know that I haven't made much effort to see the girls and I miss them. I want to be a better friend. I know how quickly things can change, so I want to make sure I do whatever I can to be a good friend.
- It's New Year and I have completed everything on my plan. That might be unrealistic now. I might need a new plan.

Success

- I think I'm doing okay, other than the small issue of being behind at Sixth Form. I have helped out at home, I didn't freak out when Mum said that Sammy was coming for Christmas and I am ready to be the model granddaughter at the weekend.

Gratitude

- Frankie. She's amazing. She's relaxed about me taking my time and not putting any pressure on me at all. Life is good, life is really good.

Twenty-Two

I'm not just avoiding Grandpa, I do have to do some work.

'Come on, you two, let's get some fresh air,' Mum says, adding to my stress. 'We can take Reggie out and work up an appetite for lunch.'

'I've got a deadline, Mum,' I say, hoping that she will be pleased I'm thinking about work and let me stay at home.

'You've always got a deadline,' she replies, and doesn't sound impressed as she knows she has been telling me for weeks that I need to make more effort with my assignments. 'Okay, you stay here but I want a full report of what you've done when we get back.'

'Sure, not that you'll understand.'

'Dani, your mother is smarter than she looks.' As soon as Grandpa says it, he knows it has come out all wrong. 'I'll get my shoes,' he mutters and he shuffles off to the kitchen.

This weekend has been the longest weekend of my life. Grandpa has been quiet and I think he'd rather be at home. He's started to find his own routine, he's seeing his friends, and there's a group of them he meets up with regularly for company. When he comes here, it's a reminder of everything that he has lost. Mum keeps talking about Christmases she remembers as a kid and I don't think it's helping.

Maybe I should go with them to change the subject and give Grandpa a break from her constant wittering. I have work to do though. I could give him Reggie's favourite ball instead so he has something to entertain him while he's out. I quickly find it and hand it to Grandpa.

'I need to make sure I don't throw it at your mother,' he whispers, putting it in his pocket before Reggie spots it.

She's getting on his nerves. I'm glad it's not just me.

When Grandpa arrived yesterday, he had bags of wrapping paper, cards and gifts. I had a sneaky look in one of the bags and hoped the book about the visual history of trains wasn't for me.

'You'll help me, won't you, love?' he asked, sounding deflated.

'Sure, what with?'

'Your grandma used to do all of this. I don't know where to start.' At that moment, I thought he was going to cry. He looked lost. He'd never had to think about presents or cards. Grandma had done everything. 'I had no idea that she did so much.'

'She loved doing all of this, so I don't think she would have let you get involved even if you'd tried to,' I said, wanting to kick myself. I sounded like Mum. I had no idea if Grandma enjoyed doing all of this. Maybe she hated shopping, doing all the wrapping up and writing all of the cards. Maybe she resented every Christmas and that Grandpa took her for granted and didn't help at all. I supposed Mum's rose-tinted-glasses approach made things a bit easier even if it was complete bollocks.

'Right, let's take it all to the living room and you can tell me who these presents are for. I'll wrap them up and you can write the tags.' I was almost glad of something to do so we weren't just drinking tea and trying to find things to talk about.

'Will you write the cards and tags too, please?'

'Jeez, what did your last slave die of.' Shit. 'I'm so sorry, Grandpa. I didn't mean that how it sounded. Sorry.' I dared to look up and saw that Grandpa was laughing at me.

'You've gone red,' he said.

'I'm really sorry. Of course, I'll write the tags and cards.' I kept apologising as I carried the bags and was grateful that Reggie joined us so we quickly had something else to focus on. That was keeping Reggie's nose out of the bags of presents, trying to get him to lie somewhere in the room that meant his tail was as far away as possible from the mugs of tea, and convincing him that none of the presents could be eaten.

Grandpa couldn't remember who he had bought half of the

presents for. 'I just wanted to get out of town as soon as I could,' he said. 'Now, who still wears ties?'

With a selection of random presents back in their carrier bags, we started on the cards. Handing me Grandma's address book Grandpa said, 'A lot of these folk are dead now, that's what happens when you get to my age.'

'Shall we start a new address book?' I offered, not expecting the reply I got.

'Nah, I need to double-check who I've crossed out sometimes so I know they're definitely dead.'

I had to laugh. What was I supposed to say to that? I couldn't imagine going through my phone and checking who was still alive. Would that be me when I was Grandpa's age? I'd have to delete people from my contacts as there wouldn't be a 'crossing out' option. Maybe there should be.

With the cards written and Grandpa sharing a story about each person I wished a Merry Christmas to, I was pleased there were so many names crossed out in that little book. There were only so many stories I could take about people I didn't know. It took us all afternoon as I was knackered. I couldn't remember the last time I'd used a pen for that long. My wrist hurt!

Mum came in as I was rubbing it. 'It just shows you need to be writing more and getting more of your work done,' she joked, seeing all our hard work.

That was my cue to escape! I hadn't done any work, but was glad of the excuse to have some time out.

Now, I do need to get on the case or I'll be panicking again. Focus, Dani, Focus.

Twenty-Three

Finally it's over. I had been looking forward to Christmas but what had started out as a fun couple of days quickly turned into a 'let's gang up on Dani' day. The only person who was sticking up for me was Sammy. What a difference a year makes! Last year, I was kicking off about him being with us for Christmas at all. This year, I don't know what I would have done without him.

It started well and we had the best Christmas lunch ever. Jane did most of the cooking with Lucy taking on the official role of 'supervisor' while Mum drank wine and Sammy was in charge of the music.

While texts were coming in from my friends about their parents arguing, their siblings fighting and being gutted that they hadn't got the latest phone upgrade, or in Katie's case, that she hadn't got a car, I was having a laugh, was excited to have awesome presents, and felt like everything was good in the world. That might have also been because Lucy kept topping up my glass with wine when Mum wasn't looking. Later I went upstairs to do some work. But was soon back down.

'It's gone blue. I don't know what to do.' I wailed as I stumbled into the living room clutching my laptop. Everyone looked at me as if I had announced I was about to die.

'What's gone blue,' asked Jane. 'You know I'm not a real doctor, don't you?' She must have been pissed. She hated it when anyone else said that. She was a 'doctor' because she had a PhD, not because she could help in a medical emergency!

'My laptop, it's gone blue. The screen just went blue.' I was about to cry. It was the worst thing that could happen. 'I've got my essays on there, I haven't saved them anywhere else. I'm not doing them all again, I can't do them all again.'

'You're not seriously telling us that you were writing essays.'

'Mum, this isn't a joke. It's blue.'

Sammy took the laptop from me and started pressing some of the keys. 'Do you even know what you're doing?' I said, pretty sure that he was just pressing things in the same way that I had.

'Leave it with me, remember, I'm the only one drinking orange juice, and fixing this means I can go and have some time out from all of these drunken women.'

'You think you can fix it?' I pleaded.

'We're not drunk, yet,' came the embarrassing shrieks from Mum and Jane. Reggie followed Sammy out of the room, no doubt grateful that someone would now be in the kitchen with the leftovers.

'It'll be okay, he'll fix it,' Lucy assured me. 'What are the essays about?'

Before I could even try to answer, Jane piped up. I was waiting for her to start, but thought she'd at least wait until Boxing Day. 'Is your Uni application on the laptop?'

There it was, the question that I was dreading. I had started the application, but I still didn't know what I wanted to do, where I wanted to go, or if I wanted to go to Uni at all.

'Yes, it's on there. Can we talk about it another time?'

'It's important, Dani. This is an exciting time, a chance to focus on what you want to do and take the next step towards being independent.' I knew there'd be no stopping her now. 'We've only got a couple of days together so let's make the most of it and figure out what your options are.'

Jane loved nothing more than talking about all of this. She was only trying to help, but it was so overwhelming that I just wanted her to shut up.

'Are you still sure about Sports Psychology being the course you want to do?'

'I don't think I've ever been "sure", have I?' I replied. 'I haven't really thought about it.'

'Would you like me to rearrange the placement for you?' she asked. I was supposed to have spent some time with her friend over the summer. She was a Sports Psychologist who Jane said could open a lot of doors for me in the future. I had been looking forward to going and learning more about what she did, but I hadn't been able to go. It had been the week of Grandma's funeral.

'Sure, that would be good.' I meant it. I still wanted to go to see what it was all about.

'If you came to a Uni near me, you could stay at mine and work with her in your spare time.' The look that Lucy gave Jane as she offered me her spare room didn't go unnoticed by any of us.

'Could I bring Reggie?' I asked, knowing that would ensure Jane never offered again.

'No,' said Mum and Jane in unison.

'Reggie is staying with me,' Mum said. Jane nodded forcefully.

'I'm staying here too then,' I said, watching Lucy breathe a sigh of relief.

'I will get that placement set up as soon as I'm home' Jane said, reaching for her diary as she knew she'd forget if she didn't write it down. She was always forgetting dates.

'Can't you leave the poor girl alone just for today,' Sammy said as he walked back in with my laptop.

'Is it fixed, please tell me it's fixed, have you fixed it?'

'It's fixed,' he proudly announced.

'Thank you, thank you, thank you,' I sang. I raced out of the room seizing the opportunity to escape while Jane was scribbling in her diary.

So now, up in my room, I need to figure out my future plans, but I have other things to focus on first.

Goals

One weekend with Jane and I'm all over this again. Even if I'm only doing it to avoid thinking about the long-term stuff, at least I'm doing it.

- It is May and I have my black tag. I only have to spend five minutes with Lucy and I want to train harder to get my black belt. She might not want me hanging around at Jane's but she's still my taekwondo heroine.
- It's New Year and I have spent time with my friends. That's going okay. I had a brilliant day with everyone in town last week and we'll be getting together before we go back to Sixth Form. They might help me figure out what to do about Uni.
- It's New Year and I have completed everything on my plan. My updated plan, that is. The updated one is a bit more realistic. Now that my screen isn't blue, I can try to get it done. Not today, but next week!

Success

- I think I have successfully made it through Christmas without any dramas. That's a good thing!

Gratitude

- Having a good day today, apart from being questioned by the fake doctor, but I knew she'd bring it all up at some point.

Twenty-Four

This is how Christmas should be. Never mind Christmas, this is how every day should be. I understand it now. I understand how people 'know' when something is right. I've heard people talk about their 'gut feeling' or 'intuition' or whatever you want to call it, but I have never really understood what they meant when they said they 'just know'.

'When I met your grandma, I just knew she was the one,' was something Grandpa said when I was writing his Christmas cards for him. I smiled and I would never have questioned it, but I had wondered 'how?' How could he 'just know?'

Now I know.

I was a bit nervous this morning on the way to Frankie's. Having our own Christmas sounded great, but I was overthinking it, worrying about it and starting to freak out a little bit. I'd stuck to my half of the deal and bought our favourite pizzas, garlic bread and ice cream. I had Reggie's rucksack, which as usual was double the size of mine. But as I knocked on the door, I wondered if it was a good idea at all.

'REGGIEEEEEEE, Happy Christmas, Dude,' Frankie welcomed cheerfully. 'I've got you a present.' I followed an excited Reggie into Frankie's house, dropping the pizza on the way, and headed for the kitchen. I heard ripping paper and the distinctive sound of a squeaky toy that would no doubt soon be de-squeaked as I unpacked the food and put the kettle on.

'You're well trained,' Frankie said from the doorway. 'I'm impressed!'

'Thanks for getting Reggie a toy, but sorry if it doesn't last very long.' I knew that it had a predicted life expectancy of about three minutes.

'It said it was indestructible,' she announced proudly, closely followed by, 'Oh, he's destroyed it.' I followed her back into the living room.

'Sorry! But I can promise you that's the best couple of minutes he's had so far today.' I felt bad, but Frankie wasn't bothered at all. She took a photo of Reggie with what was left of the toy and started unpacking his rucksack, making him a bed by the sofa, taking him some water and leaving a little biscuit for him.

'I want you both to feel welcome. Today is going to be the best Christmas ever,' she said, looking at me. She looked at Reggie and then the moment disappeared with the words, 'So, where's my present?'

I don't think I have ever laughed as much as I laughed today. We opened presents, walked to the pub for lunch and had the dubious honour of being allowed to sit in a quiet corner with Reggie so we didn't have to sit outside in the freezing cold December weather to eat. Walking back to Frankie's hand in hand, I whispered, 'Thanks for today, it's definitely the best Christmas I've ever had.'

'We're only halfway through, so it can only get better,' Frankie whispered back to me, squeezing my hand and sending a jolt through my whole body.

She was right. We watched films, curled up on the sofa and decided that when we left Sixth Form we would travel the world. Talking about the adventures we could have made it feel real – like we could actually make it happen. 'We can do anything we want to do,' Frankie promised me. In that moment, I believed her. I believed that I could do anything I wanted to do.

'It's just a shame that I don't really know what I want to do,' I joked. 'I know that right now, there's nowhere on earth I'd rather be, so that's a good start.'

I meant it. I couldn't think of a day in my whole life when I'd felt as happy and relaxed, and then it happened.

Frankie kissed me.

'I've wanted to do that since the first day we met,' Frankie admitted.

'That would have been an interesting introduction to Sixth Form PE.' I could just imagine the comments from the idiot lads in the class with us. 'I would definitely have freaked out if you'd done that instead of just saying hi.'

'Are you okay?' Frankie asked.

'I really am.'

I was surprised, but I really was okay. More than okay. I had worried about it for ages, worried that I'd be too scared to allow myself to be close to someone. I'd had nothing to worry about.

You can use whatever words you want, there might not be any words to describe it properly, but I now know exactly what people mean when they say they just 'know'.

Any element of doubt went away with that kiss. The feelings I have for Frankie have nothing to do with what happened to me, nothing at all. I was lost in the moment, I didn't want it to end and felt an indescribable wave of emotion.

Being close to someone who cares about me, who likes me for who I am and isn't scared off by my past, is the most amazing feeling in the world.

Without a doubt, today has been the best day ever. Happy Christmas!

Twenty-Five

If the start to this year is as amazing as the end of the last year, I'll be very happy.

New Year's Eve was the first time I'd celebrated properly and the first time I'd had someone to celebrate with. Mum doesn't count and in this case, Reggie doesn't really count either. I don't think he was awake when the New Year started and he definitely didn't care about what year we were in.

In fairness, I don't really care what year we're in either, but I do know that this is going to be a big year for me. I have big decisions to make and now I have Frankie to consider too. She's trying to work out what she wants to do after Sixth Form and neither of us want to plan too far ahead. Things are amazing at the moment, but it's all so new. I can't imagine my life without her right now, but I guess that's what everyone says at the beginning. I know that Mum trusted Daniel, the sperm donor, enough to start a family with him. They were living together and had made so many plans, then one day, he was gone. That was it. Never to be seen again. Jane has had her fair share of heartache over the years and even Katie now seems to have trouble in paradise. Cal didn't turn up to the party last night and was seeing in the New Year with his rugby mates instead of Katie. But what a party it turned out to be.

'I'm not bothered, we're not joined at the hip,' Katie said when we arrived there and I walked over and asked if she was okay. She obviously was bothered though. She had spent all night checking her phone and looked like she had been crying. 'I don't want to talk about it,' she snapped.

'That's fine by me, I was only going to ask if you wanted to dance,' I lied.

'Maybe later,' she said, without even looking up from her phone.

I didn't want to be in that position, staring at my phone, wishing Frankie was with me instead of out somewhere else. It was as if she had read my mind, as she came over.

'I don't want to be anywhere else on earth right now. I want to start the New Year with you,' she whispered into my ear, handing me another drink. 'Even if this is the world's weirdest party.'

Frankie was right. It was quite weird. One of Callie's friends had invited us to her house for her annual New Year's Eve party. Because Callie was a budding tattoo artist, doing really well at Art College and becoming a bit of a local legend, we thought it would be an amazing party. It wasn't.

Callie came over and dragged us off to introduce us to some of her friends. Afterwards she said, 'I don't know the others, I think they're friends of friends, but we'll have a good night anyway.'

'Who invited the snakes?' Frankie asked. Maya was hiding behind her having just spotted them too.

Across one wall of the living room were two enormous glass tanks with two equally enormous snakes. I wasn't worried about the snakes as they looked perfectly happy in their glass houses, but looking around the room, I wondered how Callie's friends lived like that. I thought I was untidy, but the room we had walked in to had taken it to a whole new level. There were clothes, mugs, dirty plates and random pieces of paper strewn everywhere. I almost tripped over a laptop on the floor as we made our way to the kitchen.

The music was loud enough to ensure we all had to shout. Katie had decided before we got there that she was going to have a rubbish night, Maya was preoccupied with her fear of snakes and Callie was drunk. I didn't care. I was determined to have a good time, and I did.

I danced, I drank and I had the weirdest, but best night out ever.

'Where do you think we'll be this time next year?' Frankie asked after the excitement of the New Year countdown was over.

'Right now, I'm just excited about where we are this year,' I replied. I couldn't think that far ahead. So much could happen and so much was going to change. 'We have to get through Sixth Form, that's the priority,' I said. 'I can't think past all those essays I have to finish tomorrow, and I reckon I'm going to have a major headache.'

I felt quite sick in the taxi home but managed to get in and up to bed without making too much noise. Mum and Sammy were nowhere to be seen but his car was outside so I tried to be extra quiet.

I woke up with that major headache I talked about.

'Good night, last night?' Mum asks when she brings me a cuppa and some toast. 'Happy New Year.'

'Yeah, not bad. Callie's friend has snakes,' I tell her.

'How much did you have to drink?' she asks.

'Seriously she has two snakes in her living room, in tanks, obviously.'

'Okay, love, maybe you should go back to sleep for a bit.' She quickly makes an exit.

I send Frankie a text to double-check that I haven't imagined the snakes. She reassures me that she saw them too.

'Thanx for last nite x,' I send to Callie. Even though the party was weird, it was still brilliant and I knew she had been a bit worried when we'd arrived.

'Nice 2 c u so happy x,' she replies.

I really am happy. It feels good. I'm not even miserable about trying to get some work done, now that's a miracle. It's been the perfect start to the New Year and now I have to make this year count for something. I'm not going to scare myself by trying to figure out what I want to do with my life, not today anyway. I'm just going to get some work done and worry about it all another day. First, I think I might take Mum's advice and go back to sleep for a bit!

Twenty-Six

I found getting up early this morning a shock to the system. Dragging myself out of bed was an effort and the walk to Sixth Form felt like a marathon. A slow marathon. The reality hit me as I was walking. It was the beginning of the end of Sixth Form. It was only a matter of weeks until all the coursework had to be finished and the exams started.

The panic overwhelmed me. It wasn't just about the exams, although that was enough to scare me back to bed so I could hide under the duvet, it was the fact I had no idea what to do next. It should have been an exciting time, where I was planning for the future – focusing on what I wanted to do for the rest of my life. Instead, I was just moving from a state of panic to a state of fear to a state of being overwhelmed approximately every two minutes.

'You must have some idea what you want to do?' Katie said when we met up in the corridor and I told her. She sounded unconvinced that I was still trying to figure things out. She had picked the degree she wanted to do at the start of last year, knew exactly what grades she needed, which Uni would be her first and second choice, and now even seemed to know which Halls of Residence she wanted to stay in. 'It's a no brainer for me,' she said. 'The one I've chosen has an en-suite, it's not like I'm going to share toilets with fifteen other students.'

She had thought it all through, while I had been avoiding it completely. She had narrowed down all the careers she wanted to do and settled on being a Physiotherapist. 'I know I said I wanted to be a doctor,' she explained, 'but it's years and years of training before you actually get to be one. If I'm a really good Physio, I'll still get to help people but I can also run my own business, work from home and have a much nicer lifestyle.'

'You really have got it all planned out, haven't you?' I was a little bit jealous while also thinking she was missing out on any sense of adventure. She'd even talked to Callie about her business logo.

'You'll wish you'd thought it through when you visit me in my big house, with my own Physio room and you're still floating around wondering what you want to do with your life.'

'Harsh!' I laughed, but the sense of panic washed over me immediately. I didn't want to be that person. I didn't want to be 'floating around', without any purpose. Katie hadn't just thought about what she wanted to do, but she had thought about all of the other aspects too. She would make a great doctor, and was definitely smart enough to get into Uni to do medicine, but she had thought beyond the career. She didn't want the lifestyle that went with being a doctor. She wanted to be her own boss, to make her money and be able to enjoy it. I could see Katie working for herself. She had the drive and motivation to get up and work, I was not sure I did.

Maya joined us. 'What are you going to do with a music degree?' I asked her, wondering if it was only Katie who had planned out her entire life.

'I'm going to teach. As long as I get into my first-choice Uni, I can study teaching alongside the degree and hopefully get a job in a good school as soon as I finish. I can teach posh kids with rich parents to help pay my way through Uni while I'm studying too!'

It really was just me who had absolutely no idea what to do. Maya had never talked about teaching, or maybe I had been so wrapped up in my own stuff that she hadn't bothered to tell me, or even worse, maybe I hadn't been listening.

'Hey, can I do work experience with your mate, pls x,' I later asked Jane in a lazy attempt to at least try to find out if I'd like Sports Psychology. Some work experience would be a good way to find out if I'd enjoy the subject, but also if I'd enjoy the lifestyle.

'Will get it sorted for half-term x,' she replied, no doubt

pleased that I had made an effort to do something.

Starting the way I mean to go on, I'm spending some time in the library. I actually quite like it in here. I can put my headphones on and concentrate while surrounded by people who are also in a mild state of panic.

The result is that I now have a plan for how I'm going to get myself the grades I need to go to Uni. I don't need to worry about exactly what I'm going to do, I have added into my plan some time to research jobs, courses and different careers. There's no point dreaming about an awesome career if I don't have the grades I need to learn about it. I won't have any choices if I fail my exams.

So, here's what I'm aiming for and I'm feeling motivated.

- It is May and I have my black tag. I have to keep focusing on that as taekwondo keeps me sane. Without exercise, I get very grumpy.
- It's half-term and I have work experience with Jane's friend sorted out. I guess that's more of a goal for Jane, but I can be ready. If I have researched loads of different careers and this is still the only one that I'm interested in, then at least I know that I need to enjoy it!
- It's half-term and I have my Uni application ready, which means I will have decided if I want to move away from home or stay here. I should probably check with Mum that she's okay with me staying at home!

Success

- Today has been seriously productive. I know what I need to do, I know that I don't have much time to do it, but I also know that it'll be totally worth it. If I know what I'm aiming for, then I'll be much more motivated to get good grades.

Gratitude

- Frankie. She is making me really happy.
- I've had the best Christmas and New Year ever, mainly thanks to Frankie!
- I'm grateful that I'm starting the New Year with a focus. Even just having these couple of hours to plan what I'm going to do has made me feel much better. I never thought I'd be grateful for the library, but there's a first time for everything.

Twenty-Seven

This evening, after a week of mock exams, I just want to lie down, watch films and hang out on the sofa with Reggie. I even put into my plan for this week that I am allowed an evening without any work so that I can relax. Frankie has another exam on Monday so she is locked away at home, revising. Callie meantime has invited us all to one of her friend's parties but I think we've all made our excuses. We've had enough of the weird parties for a while and we are all knackered after the exams.

I am aching all over thanks to the hardest taekwondo training session of my life too. Working for my black tag is fun, but it pushes me to the limit.

I've started going to training sessions early to help out with the beginners' classes. It was something that Lucy advised me to do.

'It'll help you perfect the basics, which are the foundations for everything else you'll learn,' she said. 'And it'll also remind you of just how far you've come. It's easy to forget how well you've done when you're constantly striving for the next level. Helping out a kid doing their first grading will boost your confidence and it feels good to give something back.'

At the time, I wasn't sure if I wanted to teach kids as they can be pretty annoying, but this morning, I had an amazing moment with one of the new girls, Gemma. Her mum spoke to me before the session to say that she was having a rough time at school and she hoped that taekwondo would boost her confidence.

'It worked for me,' I shared with her. 'I started training when I was having a horrible time at school and it helped me so much.'

Gemma wouldn't even look at me to begin with. She reminded me of how I used to look when I had first started. I had been frightened to say anything or look at anyone just in case the bullying started there too. It had taken a while, but thanks to everyone having been so patient and kind to me, it was soon one of my favourite places to be.

I worked with Gemma for the whole session and by the end, she was laughing, smiling and actually really good at picking up the basic moves.

'You're pretty good at this,' I said to her. 'Keep coming back and you'll get your first belt in no time.'

'You're a good teacher,' she said, looking at me properly for the first time. 'I didn't think I'd like it, but I definitely want to come back again.'

That was a real buzz. Seeing Gemma enjoy the sport that I loved so much and watching her confidence grow was amazing.

Maybe that's what Sports Psychology is? If I can get that buzz from helping people to get better at the sport they love and be more successful as a result, that will be an awesome way to spend my working days.

Just as Reggie and me settle cosily in front of the TV, Mum's voice, shatters the daydream I'm having. 'Get up, Dani, we're going for dinner.'

'Dinner? I thought you two were going out?' I am sure that Mum said she was taking Sammy for dinner so that's why I made plans to order a pizza and enjoy my big night in.

'You've worked hard this week, so we thought we'd take you out.'

Oh, all right then. Who am I to argue about being taken out for dinner?

It isn't long before I'm wishing I was back on the sofa though. Sitting in a quiet corner of our local pub, I keep seeing Mum and Sammy look at each other, as if they have something to say but don't know how to say it. I think they might have had an argument or maybe Sammy is annoyed that I've gatecrashed his night out. We're getting on much better, but I'm sure he would have preferred a night out with Mum rather than having me tag along too.

'We've noticed that you've been much happier over the last few weeks, which is great to see,' Mum says. I nod, wondering why Sammy is staring into his drink and not making eye contact with either of us. 'You've been spending a lot of time with Frankie too. Is that linked to this new, happy version of Dani that we're all enjoying?'

Before she finishes the sentence, Sammy has excused himself, muttering something about finding the gents.

'You've gone red,' Mum says, trying not to laugh but failing miserably.

'I guess the two things might be linked,' I say, copying Sammy's tactic of staring into my glass and wondering if I can hide in the gents with him.

'She's a lovely girl, you could do a lot worse.'

I want the ground to swallow me up. I can't think of anything to say but am so relieved that Mum isn't going to make a big deal out of this.

'I've known for years, love,' she whispers. 'I love you and will always support you. Just be warned though, you will be focusing on your studies first, taekwondo second, and then Frankie.'

'Are you kidding me?' I reply. 'Don't you mean, Reggie first?'

'You're right, silly me,' Mum says, raising her glass. 'Here's to happiness.' She reaches for her phone. 'I'll text Sammy to tell him he can stop hiding in the loo now.'

That was embarrassing.

Twenty-Eight

I can't sleep. I've been thinking non-stop about what Mum said.

'I've known for years.'

If she has known for years, then all those months of worrying about what I was feeling about Frankie were for nothing. I honestly thought that it might be just because I was frightened of men, even though I'm not frightened of Sammy, or Grandpa, or any of the guys at Sixth Form.

Hmmm, maybe I didn't think this through at all.

I wonder how Mum knew when I didn't. Maybe I didn't care enough to think about it. It's not like I've been inundated with offers over the last couple of years.

Before the rape, I don't remember thinking about guys at all. Some of my old friends would talk about guys they thought were fit at school or on TV. I didn't care. I didn't think the guys at school were fit. I generally thought they were idiots. When Katie started dating Cal, I was pleased for her but I couldn't see what all the fuss was about. He's a nice guy, but I think Katie put me off by the hours she spent talking about him. She's calmed down now, but she's lucky we're all still friends with her after what we had to listen to last year.

I haven't felt the urge to talk to my friends about women I thought were fit because I don't remember ever really thinking about it. Hold on. There was one teacher at my old school. She was nice! Maybe I just knew that I shouldn't announce that when I was around my old friends. She was kind to me, and helped me figure out how to remember the dates of the wars to get through a history exam. It's funny that I can still remember those dates, but can't remember anything else we learned.

Then there's Mum. She managed to figure it out.

'How did you know?' I plucked up the courage to ask her once we were back home and Sammy had left.

'Know what? Oh, that you don't want to kiss boys?'

'It's not funny!' I said, feeling like I was the adult in the house while Mum was laughing to herself.

'I remember the exact moment I knew, Dani'

'What?' I had no idea what she could be talking about. She said she had known for years so what could I possibly have done that made her so sure?

'We were out having pizza, celebrating you passing your Year Eight exams.'

Year Eight? Hold on, that was when I passed that history exam. What did I do?!

'I complained about the pizza because it wasn't what I ordered and the waitress was quite rude to me, so I asked to speak to the Manager. She was very rude, actually. You know me, I don't like to complain.'

What was she talking about? I didn't remember any of this.

'Anyway, the Manager came over and you actually looked her up and down. It was embarrassing, Dani. Admittedly, she was a beautiful woman. When she leant over to talk to us, well, let's just say there wasn't any doubt in my mind from that moment on.'

Oh. My. God.

'Stop laughing, that's not funny.' Mum was bordering on the hysterical.

'I've waited years to tell you that story,' she admitted wiping her eyes. 'You're right, it's not funny. I thought I had raised you to treat women with more respect than that.'

She was off again. I hadn't really imagined what it would be like when Mum found out I was seeing Frankie. I didn't think she'd care that she was a girl, Mum was pretty open-minded, but I hadn't expected this.

'I thought about saving that story for your wedding, but seeing your face right now is pure magic.'

'Wedding? Let's not get ahead of ourselves. There aren't any more stories you're saving are there?'

'Wouldn't you like to know.'

'YES, I bloody would.' I dreaded to think what else I might have done. 'That's so embarrassing. Who else knows about that?'

'Only Jane, and Jane's ex, and Lucy, Sammy knows and oh, Dani, it doesn't matter. That's one of the perks of having a child, you get to share the embarrassing stories. Now, I can't wait to tell Frankie. When is she coming over?'

'Never.'

'Seriously though, Dani, I don't know if you were worried about telling me or if you were worried about what I'd think. I hope you know me well enough to know that my only concern is your happiness, and I really am happy for you. Things are going your way and you have the whole world at your feet. This is an exciting time.'

'I wasn't worried about telling you, and I was pretty sure you'd be cool about me liking girls…' I stopped. I didn't know whether to say anything else.

'What is it?' Mum asked, as perceptive as ever.

'I just wasn't sure myself,' I answered, not sure whether to go into details.

'What happened to you has nothing to do with sex, nothing to do with how you feel about men or women and nothing to do with anything other than one evil piece of shit making the worst possible decision of his worthless life.'

'Well, when you put it like that.' I smiled.

'Love feels amazing, Dani. I know that's a strong word, but trust your gut. If what you're feeling for Frankie makes your heart sing, then you don't have to second-guess it. Enjoy it.'

There wasn't much I could say to that. Mum was right, it felt good and I was enjoying it. I needed to practice not to overthink things, as I was very good at that.

'Just treat Frankie with more respect that you did that

Manager.'

'Can you let that go?' I pleaded, knowing that Mum would entertain herself with that story for years now that she had shared it with me.

'Never.' She laughed.

'Marvellous.'

Twenty-Nine

'I don't get what the big deal is,' said Frankie when I told her about my conversations with Mum. 'It's not like we're in the dark ages, if you like someone you like someone, there doesn't have to be a big announcement or a label attached to it.'

'I guess I was just pleased there wasn't a drama.' I was disappointed that Frankie was being so dismissive. It was a big deal to me. It was the first time I had admitted to Mum I actually liked someone, let alone that I was officially seeing someone. That was a big deal, wasn't it? 'Have you told your folks about me?' I asked, cautiously. Frankie didn't seem to be in the mood for a deep and meaningful conversation.

'Sure, I talked about you a lot last year and then they knew I was in a bad place after everything that happened, or didn't happen, and now they know I'm happy again, because of you.'

'Are they okay with us seeing each other?' I felt like I was interviewing her. I thought this would be a laugh, something that she'd want to talk about, or at least would want to listen to after my weekend of revelations with Mum.

'Of course. I had the riot act read to me about not failing Sixth Form, but they don't care. I mean that in a nice way, they don't care that you're a girl, they just don't want me to lose focus and keep telling me how important this year is.'

'Mum said the same thing. She's worried that I'm not doing enough to keep my options open and that, if I fail, I won't have the luxury of choosing which Uni I want to go to, only which supermarket I want to stack shelves in.'

'You could do a lot worse than stacking shelves, but I don't think either of us should aim for that.' She laughed. 'I can't even think about Uni, I know that we have to figure it out, but it hurts my head. We could just run away to the circus and become a lesbian double act.'

'I thought you said that we didn't need to attach labels to anything?' I wasn't going to let that go unnoticed.

'Funny. I just meant that I don't really get the whole "coming out" thing. I mean, why make such a big deal out of it? There was a guy in my old school who spent ages planning how he was going to tell his parents, he went on and on about it. He made it into such a huge drama that he was almost disappointed when his parents didn't care. I know that some people have horrible reactions or their folks would rather lose their kids than admit to their friends they have a gay kid, but that just makes them morons and why would you want a moron in your life?'

'You make it sound so simple,' I said, wondering if she'd feel differently if she had parents who weren't so open-minded. 'We're lucky that your parents and my mum have been so cool about it, but what if you'd been rejected by the very people who should be standing by you.' I was thinking about Jane. She hadn't talked about her family and I knew that as a kid she'd spent as much time as possible with Mum and my grandparents. When she had admitted to her family she liked girls, they had told her that she was an embarrassment to them. Mum said that they were pretty horrible people anyway, but Jane being a lesbian was the icing on the cake for them. They made her life a misery and she escaped as soon as she could. How stupid was that? Jane was seriously clever, she'd gained amazing exam results, she was now a doctor and had an awesome career. She had her own house, lots of friends and was happy. Who wouldn't want that for their kid? Mum would shout it from the rooftops if I was clever enough to be called 'Doctor'.

'I suppose, but I guess it's just never been a big deal to me, or to anyone around me. I talked about women I liked when my friends talked about guys they liked. My folks have never said that their aim for me is to have a traditional two-point-four family and my dad even went and bought me extra Blu Tac when I wanted to cover my bedroom wall in posters of the Williams' sisters.'

'The tennis players? Really?' I was surprised as I couldn't be further from the muscular build of Serena and Venus, and the last time I had asked Frankie about playing tennis she had laughed at me saying she hated the sport.

'We all have our secrets, Dani!'

'You've never talked about women you like around me,' I said, wondering if I'd missed something she had said or been totally oblivious to hints she had dropped.

'It never came up in conversation.' She laughed. 'You didn't talk about anyone you liked, and I get why, but I couldn't quite figure out whether you would run into my arms or run a mile. It turned out you did both!'

'Well, we're not all as enlightened as you.'

Thinking about it now, I wasn't ready to joke about my major freak out and I didn't want to admit to Frankie that I still freak out sometimes.

We didn't talk about the future or about what we wanted to do about Uni. Frankie changed the subject with her circus comment so I didn't push it.

Shouldn't we talk about what we're going to do? I don't know if she's thinking about moving to the other end of the country, or whether she's seeing me now but thinking it's only a casual thing that she'll forget about in the summer. If I ask her, will she think I'm moving too fast or being needy? I know I'm probably overthinking things again, but if she says it's 'no big deal' once more, I'm going to have to ask her whether she's talking about us or not.

Thirty

This year is going too fast. I can't keep up and I'm getting totally stressed out about it. It's half-term next week and I have so much to do I could cry. It's not like the deadlines are a surprise, I've known about them since the first week back in January, but with everything that has been going on, I've done exactly what I promised myself I wouldn't do. I have left everything to the last minute, thinking I'd have time. I don't have time and I have no idea why I'm so bloody stupid. I always do this and I never learn from it. I'm now panicking, upsetting everyone around me and eating too much. My head is full, I can't think and Frankie hasn't helped at all.

She just sent me this message. 'Wanna stay over for Val's Day? Jus u & me x.' I've been wondering what she might say about Valentine's Day. As usual, because it is something I feel unsure about, I have avoided talking about it and thinking about it. Mum mentioned something about cooking for Sammy because restaurants double their prices so I know that I won't have the house to myself. That means I will have to go to Frankie's and I know that the 'just you and me' comment means that Reggie isn't invited. I also know what that means.

Things have been going well, but I can't help freaking out at the thought of staying over. I can't think about it. Not thinking about it is all I can think about! When Reggie is with me, I feel safe. It's not that I think Frankie would deliberately do anything to freak me out, or that Reggie would do anything other than roll over for a belly rub if she did, but when he's there, I feel protected. He's the perfect distraction if nothing else. If things are moving too fast or if I'm freaking out, I can say that Reggie needs a walk or he'll start playing with something and that gives me an excuse to shift my attention. Without him, I would have to relax about what's happening and I'm not sure if I'm ready to do that. Frankie has made a few comments about leaving him alone when he starts playing or that he's fine for another half an hour without going for a walk and I think her patience might be running out.

'Dani, get down here,' Mum shouts and her tone stops any thoughts of what might happen with Frankie.

'What have I done now?' I say as I see what she's holding and realise that I'm in trouble.

'Why didn't you tell me about this?' she asks, sticking with the tone that I know I mustn't mess with.

'Sorry, I knew you'd be annoyed and I am rewriting it now so I can resubmit it before half-term. I just didn't understand the question.' It's a poor excuse, but I'm more annoyed that I forgot to bring the pile of coursework upstairs with me. If I'd remembered to tidy up, Mum would never have known that I'd failed that essay.

'Even I understand the question, Dani. You're better than this and it's not a lack of brainpower that's led to you failing. I've been letting you get on with your life, not questioning you about your grades and look at where that's got you. You've failed, for crying out loud.'

Wow, she is not happy at all. 'It's only one piece of coursework, chill out. I'll rewrite it and it'll be fine.'

'Did you actually just tell me to chill out?'

That's it. I know I've crossed the line. Reggie gets up and leaves the room, he knows I have crossed the line too and he doesn't want to stick around for the lecture. I don't want to stick around either, but have no choice.

She goes on and on and on. Running back upstairs is a relief, but as annoying as she is, I know she has a point. I didn't want to fail that essay. I was embarrassed by what I handed in and even more embarrassed that I didn't even manage to blag a low-grade pass. I didn't need Mum to give me the extended version of her 'get your life in order' lecture, but sat through it, nodding in the right places and promising to do better.

I have learnt the hard way that it's easier to do that than try to argue because then the lecture just goes on for even longer.

I finally answer Frankie's text. 'I'd love to, but I think I'm being sent away next week x.' At least that is one less thing to worry about.

'Ur mum saw ur grade? x,' she asks, knowing that I've been dreading her finding out.

'Been having the usual lecture for the last hour x,' I reply, hoping that Frankie won't be annoyed with me too. I can't take anyone else being annoyed with me right now as I still have to get everything done.

Reggie has followed me upstairs, sensing that I need some company but has realised that now probably isn't the best time to ask me to play. He curls up under my desk, his head resting on my foot. The sound of him breathing as he sleeps is calming as I try to figure out where to start.

Mum comes up. She's brought me a drink. 'Write a list of all the things you have to do and then go in order of your deadlines,' she says. 'Please don't let yourself down. You know you can do this.'

This makes me want to cry. She believes in me and if I can just get my head around the fact that it'll be worth the effort, I know I can do it too.

Thirty-One

Being sent away to boot camp is working out well for me so far. Since I got here yesterday, I've watched films, been out for dinner and Jane's even cooked a fry-up for us.

I can get used to this, I think after we finish eating.

'Don't get used to this,' the mind reader replies. I don't know how she does it but it is really annoying. 'We're going to go and get some fresh air, walk off our breakfast and then come up with a plan to make the most of your holiday.'

'Holiday?' I reply. Is that really what Jane thinks this is? I think it's a blend of Mum wanting a break and me getting a rubbish grade, which has resulted in me being sent away from the distractions of Frankie and my friends. Mainly Frankie. Actually, it's only Frankie as my friends have been working hard and getting good grades, not that I've shared that with Mum.

'Would you be getting a lie-in and a fry-up at home? No, I thought not. This is a holiday and you're going to enjoy it,' Jane tells me.

'Sure, a homework holiday is what everyone dreams of,' I reply. 'There's nothing like some enforced fun, and I'm ready for a nap after that breakfast.'

'It's not just homework, Dani. We're going to be talking about the Uni application too. You can't keep avoiding it and I know you must have been thinking about what you'd like to do next.'

'I really haven't,' I say, honestly. 'I mean, I know I should be thinking about and I know I'm running out of time, but there's too much to think about it, and I don't even know for sure what I want to do, whether I even want to go to Uni or whether I need to do something different.'

'You'll have a better idea about Sports Psychology by the end of the week, so that'll be a good start.'

Jane has arranged for me to spend a couple of days with her

friend so I can find out what a Sports Psychologist actually does. I'm looking forward to it, but if I don't like it, I'm totally back to square one as I have no idea what else I want to do. As soon as I start thinking about it, my heart races, my head feels full and I can't make sense of it. There's something blocking me from thinking about it.

'Come on, let's work off some of that stodge,' Jane says. She throws me my jacket and reaches for her keys.

'It's weird going for a walk without Reggie,' I say, not completely sure I mean to say it out loud.

'Humans can go for walks too. It's not all about Reggie.'

Jane has never been Reggie's biggest fan, but I think a walk is one hundred times more fun with him than just with another human. He doesn't make me think about the future. He doesn't make me talk about what I want to do with my life. Weirdly, he's probably also the only living creature I have actually talked to about it all. I sat with him in the park a couple of weeks ago, and as he came bounding towards me, carrying his soggy tennis ball and looking at me as if I was the most important person in the world, I said, 'I can't go away to Uni. I can't leave you.' It wasn't like he understood, but my eyes filled up, preparing to leak tears. He dropped his ball and put his paw on my knee. If I was being sentimental, I would have said he was in tune with how I was feeling and wanted to comfort me. In reality, I think he just wanted me to throw the ball again.

Either way, he is my lifeline and I can't leave him. I just don't think I can admit that to Jane without her thinking I'm insane.

'It's always all about Reggie,' I joke, testing her response, but she rolls her eyes. Nope, I don't think she understands at all.

'What's scaring you about making a decision?' Jane asks as we walk towards the town. She never warms up into the big questions; she just hits me with them.

'Jeez, and you wonder why I think it's better to walk with Reggie?' My attempt to avoid the question is met with silence.

Jane waits for me to reply and I have no idea where to start. 'I don't know if I want to move away but I also don't know if I want to stay at home. I'm sure Mum would like to have the place to herself so she can move Sammy in. I don't know what I want to do with my life, so trying to figure all of this out is doing my head in.' I'm getting annoyed. If I knew what to do, I'd obviously be doing it.

'How much of this uncertainty is linked to Frankie?' she asks. I knew she would bring this up at some point and I am ready to be completely honest.

'Not as much as you and Mum think.' I know that they have been talking about it. 'I'm happy and I really love Frankie. But I need to figure out what I want to do and hope it all works out.'

'That's very sensible.' Jane sounds surprised. 'So, what's the big deal about going to Uni, the one with the best Sports Psychology course has a great campus, loads going on and you can come home at weekends if you want to.'

'You really don't get it,' I whisper, close to tears. 'I don't feel safe when I'm not at home.'

'What do you mean? You feel safe at my house, don't you?' Jane seems genuinely surprised at what I've just said. Jane, of all people.

'Not when you're not there. No I don't,' I admit. Jane only went out to the shops yesterday and I had a minor panic when I thought I heard a knock at the door. It was a delivery driver knocking on next door's window, and still my heart was pounding. I knew it didn't make any sense and that it was irrational to be frightened, but my brain had responded before my logic could kick in.

'You're quite often at home by yourself when your mum's at work or at Sammy's…' Jane figures out the reason why I feel safe halfway through the sentence. 'You're not on your own, are you?' Finally, she starts to understand. 'That bloody dog is with you.'

'That bloody dog makes me feel safe,' I say, my eyes filling up.

'Okay, so we need to think about this because you can't spend your days with Reggie as your only sidekick, and I want you to feel safe. I want you to be able to make choices based on what you want and I really want you to feel safe in my home. I'd no idea.' Admitting this must be painful for Jane as she usually knows me better than I know myself. 'I'm sorry, we'll figure this out.'

'You don't have to fix anything,' I say. 'Just understand that Reggie is a huge part of my life and a huge part of why I'm doing okay. I know that I need to base my choices on more than him, but if I don't feel safe, I can't function. With him, I feel completely safe.' I can almost smell the burning as Jane's brain goes into overdrive and know exactly what she is going to say next, before she utters the words.

'Let's get a cuppa.' These are the words that fix everything according to Jane and my mum. Heading into the café, I know that the conversation is far from being over.

Thirty-Two

I've only been doing it for two days, and I'm knackered. Getting up and going to work is exhausting. I'm not even doing any work, I'm just watching Seema work.

When I started yesterday I discovered that Seema went to Uni with Jane and had decided quite early on that she wanted to focus on Sports Psychology rather than 'the energy draining stuff' as she called it. She made me laugh as after almost everything she said, she added, 'Don't tell Jane I said that.'

I didn't think Jane would like some of what she said, which was probably why I found it so funny.

'Working with sportspeople means that I spend every day with people who're trying to be the best that they can be,' she said, full of energy and passion for her work. 'They aren't wallowing in self-pity and, believe me, many of them have had a really tough time. They wake up every day and try to be better than they were yesterday.'

'You really enjoy this, don't you?' I asked.

'Of course, what's the point in getting up and doing something that doesn't make you happy? It's not always easy and there's still boring paperwork and the occasional idiot to deal with, but spending my days with people who are genuinely passionate about what they're doing is inspiring. I couldn't do what Jane does. She spends her days with people who are stuck in a cycle of misery, and while she does amazing work – you can tell her I said that – I think I'd go home every day wanting to cry. In this job, I go home buzzing.'

'I've never met anyone who talks about their work like this,' I said, genuinely surprised that someone could feel this way about their job. 'I mean, I know Jane loves what she does and I have no doubt she's really good at it, but she's not excited about it. My mum also spends every weekday wishing it was Friday and then starts complaining about work again on a Sunday afternoon.'

'I think that's how a lot of people feel, Dani. It makes me sad. I think it's great that you're not rushing into a decision and you're coming to see what really happens in this line of work. Don't settle for something you're not passionate about. Tell me, if you could change one thing in the world, what would it be?'

Wow, there was a question. I shocked myself with how easily I answered it. 'I want people to know that whatever they have been through, they can still be whoever they want to be and that life really can be amazing.'

'That's an incredible mission, Dani. That's going to be your life's work. Did you notice how you changed as you said those words? Your eyes lit up, you were excited and I believed every word. I feel motivated just by listening to you. So, what do you do in your life at the moment that brings you the most happiness?

That was easy. 'Spend time with my dog, spend time with my friends, and I feel I'm in the right place when I train. I do taekwondo.'

'Jane said not to mess with you and that you're almost a black belt,' Seema joked. 'So, sport makes you come to life, so you'll be at home spending your days with people who feel the same way as you do. People who know that sport's the answer, even if they've no idea what the question is. Your friends will always be there, and by working in an environment that's filled with like-minded people, you easily find new friends. You might not like everyone, but you'll respect most them. Then there's the dog. I know people who have their dog with them when they have consultations, a lot of the clients find it easier to relax and talk when there's a dog in the room.'

'This is my dream job then, isn't it?' I said, feeling I might have found the thing I could happily spend my days doing.

'I've no idea, but I do know you could make it work for you, and that the lifestyle you're looking for can be found in this work.'

I can't stop thinking about it all. The couple of days I've spent with Seema have inspired me and have made me want to think about my future. I want to go to Uni and study Sports Psychology. I want to make it work for me and I am finally excited about it. I am also knackered, but in a good way. My brain has been working, but it has been working on something I do feel passionate about. I wouldn't mind coming home and feeling tired if it felt like this. Now, I need to figure out how I can make it happen.

Thirty-Three

'Did Seema slip you some of those energy drinks she loves so much?' Jane asked earlier this evening when she found me at her kitchen table, already working.

'Better than that, she slipped me my dream job,' I replied. 'Did I tell you I met an Olympic medallist?'

'Three times.' Jane rolled her eyes but didn't look fed up at hearing me being excited by my work experience.

'It didn't feel like work at all, it was amazing.'

'That's probably because you weren't actually doing any of the work, Dani.'

'Okay, that's a good point, but Seema didn't look like she was working either, she looked like she was having fun.' I stopped myself. I knew that if I got too excited about it, Jane would start her lecture about how I should take all of it seriously and how it was not always about fun.

'You could do a lot worse than getting paid to have fun.' That shocked me. Maybe I was being unfair to Jane. 'Now we need to get back to reality and think about how you'll get yourself to Seema's position in a few years' time. Or better still, to become Seema's boss.'

'That would be cool, and then I could ask her to make me my tea, like she did to me.'

'No wonder she was having so much fun.' Jane picked up her notepad and pen so I knew she meant business. She sat down opposite me and it was clear the fun was over. 'Let's figure this out. Then, Lucy is coming to take you to her training session and if you want, I'll take you for a drive later.'

'You mean, with me driving?' I asked hopefully. My lessons were going okay but I was still too scared to book a test date.

'Yes, with you driving! Is that enough motivation to get you to focus on this for a little while?'

'Taekwondo and driving? Sure! Throw in some pizza and you will have my undivided attention.' I knew I was pushing my luck, but it was worth a try. I only had two more days at boot camp and I knew Jane used me as an excuse to get takeaways.

'Deal.'

That was easier than I thought and I was actually looking forward to working out how I could turn into Seema. Well, not literally, although she was pretty cool.

'Are you sure you want to apply for Sports Psychology?'

Jane had an annoying habit of making me second-guess my decisions. For once, I felt sure. I also knew that if I got to Uni and hated it, I could try to change courses. Seema did, so it's not like I was totally stuck for the rest of my life. I just had to go with what felt right. Working with Seema felt right, so that had got to be a good start. 'I'm sure,' I said, more enthusiastically than I would have liked, as Jane thought I was taking the piss.

'This is serious, Dani, this is a big decision.'

'I know, I'm sure. I really am. It's the first time I've felt sure about any of this.' I surprised myself by how sure I was. As Jane was asking me about it, I became more certain. It felt good to have made that decision as now I knew what I was aiming for. All I needed to do, was figure out how to get there.

'There are a lot of options to consider now.' Jane put down her pen, pushed her glasses up her nose and looked like she was about to deliver some bad news. 'How about, we go for the option that will give you as many choices as possible when you pick up your results?'

Now she had my attention. 'What do you mean?' I asked, wondering if this meant there was a magical solution that I hadn't thought of, a way to feel safe and still go to Uni, a way to make the permanent headache of uncertainty go away.

'Your focus has to be on getting the best grades possible so that when the time comes to make a final decision about where you go and when you go, you still have choices and you're not forced into a path you're not happy with.'

'Sounds good.' I wasn't sure where Jane was going with this. She had been so determined to find a clear path for my future that this was sounding weird, coming from her.

'In order to work hard and get your grades this year, you need to feel safe. I don't just mean safe in terms of being at home with Reggie, but safe in the knowledge that you have choices and that you won't ever be forced to make a decision you're not comfortable with.'

I could see that Jane was getting upset.

'I'm sorry that I've put pressure on you. I've been so busy trying to make you see that you're capable of doing anything you want to do with your life, that I forgot the most important thing. Feeling pressured into making a decision is the worst possible scenario for you.'

'It's okay, I know you're trying to help,' I said, not wanting Jane to feel bad about any of it. She was one of the few people who had always been there for me and I knew that. Annoying as she could be, she would never want to upset me.

'Now that you know you want to do Sports Psychology, why don't you apply for the best Uni, the most local Uni, and any others that you like the look of. Then, you're keeping your options open and it will be down to them to decide if they want to offer you a place. If you get the grades and decide that you need to apply again, not that I can imagine anyone turning you down, you can take a gap year or be an intern for Seema, anything, but you're not bringing Reggie here.'

In a heartbeat, all of the pressure was lifted. I knew what I wanted to do, but there wasn't just one route that I needed to take to get there. I had options, I had choices and I only had to take one step right away. I only had to fill in the form and then I could concentrate on Sixth Form while I let the universities decide if they wanted me or not.

'You might feel differently in the summer and so you will

still have different options,' Jane said. I knew she hoped I'd decide to go to the Uni with the best course, But I was sure she'd understand if I stayed at home and went to the local Uni too.

'So, I just need to fill in the form,' I said, making it sound simple. 'Will you help me with my personal statement?' I knew that was going to be a nightmare.

'After pizza?'

'Most definitely,' I agreed. It was nice to know that it wasn't just me who procrastinated.

Thirty-Four

Boot camp already feels like a lifetime ago. I was on a mission, working hard and feeling as if I knew where I was heading. It is much harder to keep that focus and motivation now I'm back at home.

Jane kept a close check on me while I was away.

'You're still writing down your goals, aren't you?' she asked me at one point, although she must have known the answer. 'I bet you feel more focused and productive when you're writing them down every day.'

She was right, of course. I do feel better when I do it, I just forget. I guess my goals have changed a bit now too. My big goal is to go to Uni to study Sports Psychology. Or is it? Is my big goal to be a Sports Psychologist and Uni just a stepping-stone to that? Either way, I have to get through Sixth Form or I won't be doing either of those things.

On one of the days I trained with Lucy, I was buzzing and was ready to take on the world. I then wrote one of my assignments in record time and had a draft of my personal statement finished, ready for Jane to delete and re-write!

'It's a good start,' she offered, after she'd read it, while her finger hovered over the delete button. 'Would you like me to tweak it?'

'I would love nothing more,' I said, crashing on the sofa, knowing that she would turn it into a literary masterpiece.

She did turn it into something special and I returned home up to date with all my work, with essays ready to hand in and the now infamous university application form submitted. I did exactly what Jane suggested. I applied for the best course, the most local course, and then based the others on how close they were to home or Jane. I probably could have done more research, found out more about the courses or tried to figure out if I was ready to leave home, but I was comfortable with my reasons for applying and was not worrying about it anymore. I just needed to get it done.

'I can't believe you've done all of that,' Mum said when I told her. She sounded as if she actually didn't believe it, which was annoying.

'Want to read my application?' I offered, knowing she would be impressed. 'Jane made me sound like a living legend in the personal statement.'

There were raised eyebrows as Mum said, 'She really does have a way with words, doesn't she?'

'I know. The weird thing is that it's all true, but she makes it sound so much better than it is.' I knew that my first draft was a poor effort in comparison, but I could never write like that.

'She really does.' I wasn't expecting Mum to be quite so honest about that. 'So, what are you up to now that you have a weekend free of deadlines before getting back to reality on Monday?'

I shrugged and went back up to my room. I had been avoiding that question myself.

Frankie just sent me a message. 'Wanna stay over 4 a welcome back weekend? x.'

I enjoyed the week away. We were in contact every day, but I enjoyed the pressure-free break. With that one message, it all comes flooding back.

I think it's zapped my motivation even more as my mind is racing. I do want to see her, of course I do. I'm just not sure I want to stay over.

I look at myself in the mirror. It's not something I usually do, mainly because most of the time I'm running late, but I still don't feel comfortable with what I see. I have lost the comfort-eating weight I gained when I moved here, and thanks to a combination of taekwondo and walking a super-energetic hound, I look okay. Nobody else has seen me like this though. I used worry about what I looked like, I ate so many Jaffa Cakes there was a risk I would turn into one, but now I'm worrying about it in a different way. Am I ready for Frankie to see me, all of me, and am I ready to trust her in this way?

There's only one way to find out, I suppose. I can always come home again. 'Sure, sounds good,' I reply, trying to remain as relaxed as possible. Now I need to think about something else before I find my way to the biscuit tin.

Goals

- It is May and I have my black tag. I am definitely a step closer thanks to Lucie kicking my ass last week.
- It's Easter and I am up to date with all of my Sixth Form work! The goals I set myself a few weeks ago have actually been achieved, which is a pretty cool feeling. I have done the work experience, have met my deadlines and submitted my Uni application.

Success

- That I am on track and not spending the weekend writing essays while panicking and crying. I almost don't know what to do with myself.
- Replying to Frankie and not freaking out completely. I only freaked out a little bit!

Gratitude

- Jane helping me get my life in order and it turns out I do feel like I've had a holiday.
- Frankie wanting to see me. Despite my little freak out, I'm lucky that someone wants to spend time with me.
- Having a lie-in and a morning with my favourite boy.

Thirty-Five

Last night was an emotional rollercoaster. It certainly taught me a lesson, too. I was getting ready to go to Frankie's, a bit worried that I hadn't heard from her all afternoon, but I figured she was getting ready for us to spend some time together. I messaged her a picture of Reggie looking sad as he watched me pack my bag. He seemed to know that he wasn't invited. Usually she replied straight away, but I hadn't heard from her for a couple of hours.

I knew that I hadn't done anything to upset her, but my mind was starting to play games with me. Had she changed her mind? Would she rather not see me? Was she trying to work out how to tell me not to come over? I hated it when I overthought everything.

Just as Mum shouted that she was ready to give me a lift, my phone beeped. 'So, so soz, babe. Gutted but been sick all afternoon. Mum's staying here to look after me. So soz x.'

My first thought should have been concern that Frankie was poorly, but it wasn't. I was gutted that I wouldn't get to see her and stay over. I sat on my bed, replying and telling her I hoped she would feel better soon, then immediately sent another message saying, 'I'm gutted too x,' which was the truth.

Maybe I wasn't as freaked out as I thought I was; maybe I was ready to trust Frankie? I wasn't to find out this weekend though and waking up in my own room this morning, I was disappointed not to be waking up with Frankie.

'Let's not waste the day,' Mum said, as she made us breakfast. 'I've said we'll go out for a walk and have a late lunch with Amie.'

That wasn't one of my new plans for the day, but I figured it would be good to see Amie. Frankie was still locked away in her bathroom so I wouldn't be seeing her for a while.

I had been planning to kick and punch my way through a stack of pillows in an attempt to practice before tonight's training session, but the fresh air would do me good. Lunch would do me good too!

As usual, when we got there, it took at least ten minutes for Amie even to say 'hi' to me. She adored Reggie and the feeling was mutual, so as soon as they spotted each other at the park there was a lot of squealing, bouncing around, and cuddles. I waited patiently for them both to calm down while our mums sat on the nearest bench, where they would probably stay until we left to go for lunch.

'You two go and take him for a stretch while we catch up,' Mum told me, reaching for her flask of tea and the two mugs she had packed. She hadn't brought four mugs so it was clear that Amie and I weren't going to be included in the catch up, even though there was no doubt we would be discussed.

'We don't want you cramping our style anyway,' Amie shouted as she ran off, racing Reggie to his tennis ball which was never going to end well. I raced after her. 'I swear he gets quicker every time I see him,' she said when she stopped, out of breath. She bent over to try to recover.

'I swear you get slower,' I replied, throwing the ball again. 'How are you doing, apart from being unfit and knackered?'

'Never mind me. I'm fine, what about you?' She looked at me suspiciously, as if there was a hidden meaning to her question.

'I'm good, thanks. I've been at Jane's and am almost ready to face Sixth Form again.' Amie was smirking as I answered, but I couldn't figure out why.

'You look really happy,' she said. 'What's her name, like I have to ask?'

'Oh, so that's why you're smirking. Who told you?' I didn't need to ask, I knew that our mums talked on the phone every week.

'I'm upset you didn't tell me, but it's cool to see you so happy. Does Reggie like her? I won't have anyone upsetting him.' I swore that Reggie captured the heart of almost everyone he met. Amie sounded genuinely concerned that Reggie was happy with the new person in his life.

'Of course, like I'd want to be with anyone who didn't like him,' I said honestly. 'Don't worry though, you're his favourite.' That was true too. There was only a handful of people that he was that excited to see.

'I think it's cool that you've found someone. I mean, it's not like I was surprised, you talked about Frankie in a different way to your other friends.'

It was a good day and Amie wasn't the first person to tell me that. It seemed the only person who needed to think it all through was me.

So, I missed Frankie today, but I think the week away and now the relaxed weekend has been good for me. I have a few weeks to stay on track before Easter and as long as I don't let the deadlines creep up on me, I'll be able to enjoy more time with Frankie without getting stressed out. If I can keep feeling like this, I'll be flying.

Goals

- It is May and I have my black tag.
- It's Easter and I am up to date with all of my Sixth Form work.

Success

- Nothing much today, other than getting out of the house and enjoying myself.

Gratitude

- A day with Amie, which is always good for my soul.
- Amie being so cool about me seeing Frankie, not that I would have expected anything else from her.
- Feeling ready to get back on the case with Sixth Form tomorrow and catching up with my friends.

Thirty-Six

The week started so well, and then today I came crashing back down to earth with a bang. Frankie wasn't in Sixth Form for a couple of days, which meant I was more productive than usual and had a good time catching up with Maya and Katie.

They were impressed that I finally decided on my Uni plan.

'I can see you being a successful Sports Psycho,' Maya said, when I excitedly told them both all about my couple of days with Seema.

'Psychologist,' I corrected her, thinking that my business cards wouldn't be quite as impressive as Seema's with that title.

'I prefer "Psycho", I think it suits you,' she stated, looking like she had given it some thought.

I moved on as quickly as possible, and it felt good to be able to talk to them about making the decision and being up to date with everything. Usually, they were talking about the essays they were working on while I was still panicking about the ones that were overdue. I actually enjoyed having lunch with them without feeling overwhelmed and as if I was wasting time when I should be in the library. Not that spending time with my friends was ever a waste of time, but I hadn't enjoyed it in a while because I'd been too busy panicking.

The day had gone well. I'd learnt something from it. I just needed to remember that panicking was not fun, and all I had to do was stay on top of my deadlines. I didn't think it could be that difficult. I was doing okay, it had only been two days and I'd only been given one piece of work to complete, but I guessed even I would be able to manage that without a drama. We didn't have long left until we went on study leave, which was scary and exciting all at the same time. So life wasn't at all bad.

But that was then. It was earlier today, when things began to go wrong. I should have known it was too good to be true.

'I've got a countdown by my desk and every night I cross out another date,' Katie told us over lunch. She was desperate to leave Sixth Form and get on with her plan to be super-successful.

'Like you see with people in prison?' I asked, remembering a film I had watched a while ago where a guy was counting down the days until his release.

'Don't you feel like we're in prison?' she asked. 'We're stuck here, day in day out, just ticking off the days until we can actually start learning something useful that will help us to build a career.'

'Are you okay? This isn't like you.' I was surprised that Katie was on such a downer, she was usually the person motivating us.

'Cal's decided that we need to take a break and have some time out from each other,' she whispered. 'We haven't split up,' she added with more volume and feeling. 'We're just having some time to ourselves.'

'Wow, I'd no idea, I'm really sorry,' I said, but before I could finish what I was going to say she cut in.

'There's nothing to be sorry about, we haven't split up, it's fine. I'm late, I'm going to waste another hour of my life learning about nothing.' With that, she threw her bag over her shoulder and disappeared into the crowded hallway.

'Oh yeah, she's totally fine,' Maya said as I contemplated going after her. 'Let's hope they don't split up as I don't think any of us are ready to deal with Katie in that sort of mood.'

'Do you think they might?' I asked, feeling bad that I hadn't realised what was going on with Katie. I had been so focused on my own stuff that I hadn't asked about her and Cal.

'No idea.' Maya shrugged. 'And to be honest, I'm not sure I care.'

'Are you okay?' I asked, now feeling like I had managed to miss everything that was going on in my friends' lives.

'Yeah, just fed up and can't wait to get out of here. I thought it'd be a fun couple of years hanging out with friends and not having the strict rules of school. Turns out, my friends have fallen in love and I almost miss the rules of our last school as it meant I wasn't sitting on my own trying to motivate myself.'

'Shit. I'm so sorry. I had no idea. I don't want to be that person and I'm sorry.' I couldn't believe what Maya was saying. I felt awful and she left me sitting by myself, as she moved onto her next class with a shrug.

'That's life, I guess,' she called back over her shoulder.

I was feeling like the worst friend on earth when I spotted Frankie walking through the hallway towards my table. I wasn't sure if she'd be back yet and I didn't think I'd ever been as relieved to see her as I was in that moment.

She walked towards me, saying, 'Don't worry, I'm not contagious.' She gave me a hug that instantly cheered me up.

I went from feeling so guilty I could cry, to the relief of seeing Frankie, and then back to guilt in a split second. Because as we broke away from our hug, one of the guys from our PE class walked past and shouted 'dykes', then laughed with his friends. Frankie swore at him and I sat back down, knowing that I wouldn't be going to the PE class the following day.

'Ignore him,' Frankie said, and she started giving me the details of her recuperation as if that word had never been shouted.

I listened to her; at least, I tried to. My brain had gone into overdrive though. It was replaying all of the memories I had tried to bury from Year Eleven, where the bullies would torment me with that word amongst other things. I was smiling and nodding as Frankie spoke, but I knew that I just had to get home. In the space of ten minutes, the longest ten minutes I've experienced in months, I went from being relieved to seeing Frankie, to being relieved that we had different classes to go to.

'See you tomorrow, I've got training tonight,' I said as she walked to her class. I started walking in the direction of mine, but as soon as she was out of sight, I turned around and walked the other way. I couldn't sit in class and concentrate. I went home, ran upstairs and cried.

Thirty-Seven

I didn't train, I didn't do any work and instead I walked Reggie to the local shop so that I could buy more Jaffa Cakes.

'I've got some friends coming over,' I lied as the guy served me. I'm pretty sure people only say that when it's a lie. Why would he care whether I had friends coming over or not?

Mum was having dinner at Sammy's so I didn't have to explain myself and by the time she came home, she wasn't surprised to find me in bed.

'Goodnight,' she whispered into my dark room. She called Reggie to take him back downstairs.

The rule that he wasn't allowed in my room had never worked out, but she still did her best to get him to sleep on his bed downstairs, rather than on my bedroom floor. He couldn't do anything quietly so I heard his wagging tail knock over my folders and then his heavyweight effort of getting down each stair with Mum telling him to be quiet, as if that would make a difference.

'I thought today was an early start,' Mum said as she was leaving for work today and I was still in my pyjamas.

'No, that's tomorrow,' I lied. 'Now that we're almost at study leave, some things get moved around so we can finish coursework.'

'Okay, well, have a good day,' she called out. She was obviously running late and not really listening. That was fine by me. I couldn't face explaining why I wasn't going to Sixth Form.

'My stomach has come out in sympathy with yours. x,' I messaged Frankie. Another lie. That was three in under twelve hours and I did not feel good about it.

'Nooooooooo, sending get-well vibes x,' she replied. I realised she'd already forgotten about what had happened yesterday.

Once she'd shouted back, that seemed to be the end of it as far as she had been concerned.

I know that she was pissed off about it, but I wish I had her ability to forget about it and move on.

I spent last evening feeling awful about being such a bad friend and being too scared to go to Sixth Form today because there was no way I was going to face those guys in PE. I bet today they've forgotten about it too. They're actually okay most of the time, I've worked with some of them on different projects and they're good fun. I bet they thought they were joking, and that we'd laugh it off. They call everything 'banter' and I have no doubt they'd say exactly the same about this. Except, it's not 'banter' to me, it hurt and I can't face going back to being frightened every day. Frightened it will happen again, frightened it will get worse; it's exhausting and already I have let them get the better of me.

Last night, I was second guessing everything. This is what happens when I don't do the things that I know will help me and instead, do the exact opposite. I knew training would help, but I didn't go. I knew that finishing my assignment would help, but I didn't even switch on my laptop. I knew that a long walk with Reggie would help, but the poor dude only had a half an hour walk and he made me feel bad as we turned the corner to come home, instead of carrying on to the park. He stopped, looked in the direction of the park and then looked at me. 'Not today,' I said, and felt even worse.

I convinced myself that Frankie hadn't really been ill and that she had been using it as an excuse not to see me. I convinced myself that Katie and Maya had been talking about what a horrible person I was because I hadn't made the time to see them. I cried as I sent apologetic messages and cried even more when they told me everything was fine and we'd catch up properly soon. I cried when Frankie sent me a funny video link with a dog that looked like Reggie, and tried to remember that she did like me and she did want to see me.

I cried as I remembered all of the things the bullies said to me. That one word had opened the floodgate of memories and I couldn't close it.

Maybe that's what I needed: a good cry. Today, more than any other feeling, I'm disappointed with myself. I know what I need to do to sort my head out and I've chosen not to do any of them. Today, now that I've already lied, I have a choice. I can spend the day feeling as crappy as I did last night, or I can give myself today to sort myself out again. I can practice, ready for training tonight, I can finish my assignment and I can get back to Sixth Form tomorrow and be a good friend, see Frankie and get back to class.

Even writing this down is making me feel stronger and motivated. The first thing I'm going to do is make it up to Reggie and take him to the park. Nobody will see me as they're all in class, where I should be. I'm allowed a 'blip day' as Jane sometimes calls them. As long as I can get myself out of it, I'm allowed. As long as I stick to my new plan for today, this will be a record for me in getting myself sorted out after such a downer.

Goals

- It is May and I have my black tag. Missing one training session isn't great, but I can make up for it and work extra hard tonight.
- It's Easter and I am up to date with all of my Sixth Form work. Only one little assignment and I'll be back on track. I can catch up on today's lessons, but definitely can't miss any more.

Success

- Not starting the day by eating more Jaffa Cakes.
- Being able to talk myself out of the 'blip'.

Gratitude

- The messages from Katie & Maya. I think it was just a bad day for all of us yesterday but I do need to be a better friend and make more effort.

Thirty-Eight

It's easy to forget how far I've come. It wasn't so long ago that I would have struggled to get myself out of that black hole. It would have been days, or weeks, not hours before I was back in the land of the living. I would have been stuffing my face with junk food, wallowing and going over and over how unfair life is until it would have felt almost impossible to get out of bed.

Life is unfair. I get that now and it's a lot easier to deal with now that I'm not expecting things to be a different way. What I have learnt though, is for every black hole, there's a rainbow waiting for me – literally in my case!

After my allocated 'blip day', I did pick myself up, I finished my assignment and I went training. I admit, when I got home I celebrated with ice cream, but that's okay, I earned it.

I went back to Sixth Form and walked into the PE class with some nerves, but with a higher purpose. Those idiots would not stand in the way of me passing this course and getting to Uni.

'All right?' said one of the idiots as he held the classroom door open for me.

'When did you turn into a gentleman?' I asked, making sure I didn't show any signs that I was still nervous, even though my palms started sweating and my heart was racing as he made eye contact with me.

'I'm a nice guy' he said, sounding offended. 'You just need to get to know me.'

'I'll take your word for it,' I replied. That was more than enough conversation with him for one day but he walked away smiling and without calling me any names so I felt better.

Frankie raced in, just in time, as our teacher was on the warpath. Most people were late with their assignment, Frankie being one of them, and as he launched into his lecture about how important these few weeks were, blah, blah, blah, I was able to sit back and enjoy the tired, defeated expressions on the faces of my peers, knowing I'd handed my assignment in.

'Smug is not a good look,' Frankie whispered.

'Don't worry, it won't last long,' I admitted.

I also spoke to Frankie about needing to spend more time with my friends. They're our friends really, I guess, but I wanted to make sure we could still enjoy time as a group. I hadn't thought much about how I would make that happen, but Frankie obviously listened more than I gave her credit for.

'How 'bout we work all day an' go out all day tomoz? Pizza n town? x,' her text message read yesterday morning. It was a great idea, but I wanted to see my friends too. I heard my phone beep again straight after and realised it was a group message. Frankie had invited all of them.

'Amazing idea, can't wait till tomoz x,' I replied to everyone and then sent 'thank you x' to Frankie. I knew that she'd done that for me. Knowing that I had a whole day with all my friends to look forward to was all the motivation I needed.

So, assignments were written, pillows were kicked and punched, my driving lesson was completed (with one embarrassing stall at a busy roundabout but we'll forget that happened) and I even cooked dinner for Mum and me. Pasta and garlic bread counts as cooking for me.

'What have I done to deserve this?' Mum asked, kindly not mentioning the overcooked pasta and rock hard bread.

'Just trying to be nice' I said, quickly followed by, 'I'm going out with everyone into town tomorrow.'

'There we go.' Mum laughed. 'I'll search my purse for some pennies in the morning.'

'Thank you!'

Thinking about the last few days has been a wakeup call. Maybe

I'm not as frightened as I thought I was. Maybe I am more capable of facing my fears than I thought I was. Everyone has bad days, I know that. Mine are just often accompanied by some horrible memories. The memories don't just affect my mind, they affect my body too, and that combination can be hard to work through. I did though; I went from being under the duvet, to facing my fear of walking into the classroom where I knew I'd see that idiot again.

Except, he's not really an idiot, he just did something that hurt me. Then, he did something nice. Maybe he was having a bad day too.

I'd gone from that incident, to having the best day with my friends.

Sharing it with Frankie was perfect. She managed to motivate all of us and we spent a lot of time congratulating ourselves on working hard so that we could enjoy some time together. We ate, we laughed and in our excitement Maya shouted, 'We should book a holiday.'

'Yeah, let's do it,' Katie joined in, while I could feel my nerves rising even though I was desperate to join in.

'I'm serious,' Maya continued. 'If spending one day in town got us all working, just think what a holiday will motivate us to do.'

She had a point. Looking around, I could see the wave of excitement washing over everyone. Locations were being shouted, the volume was ridiculous and it suddenly dawned on me.

'I don't even have a passport' I said.

'That's an easy problem to fix,' Frankie told me. 'Where do you want to go?'

I had absolutely no idea, I didn't really care. I sat back and watched as I knew I wouldn't get a word in edgeways. It was fun to be a part of this, to have a group of friends and for them to want me to be a part of this. In that moment, I realised I felt safe with them. I could go on holiday, have an adventure and know that they'd look out for me, and that I'd look out for them.

Today I remembered the words of one of the police officers who helped me during the court case. We were sitting outside the courtroom, drinking the most disgusting hot chocolate I had ever tasted. 'One day, sooner than you think, you'll be sitting around, laughing and enjoying yourself. There'll be a moment when you realise that you really are more than okay, and that you've made your way through this, and you're out the other side.'

At that time, I hadn't believed it was possible. Now, I want to call and tell her that she was right and that moment is now.

Thirty-Nine

I don't think life gets much better than this.

I've been sent upstairs to get ready as Mum is taking me out for a shopping trip and some lunch. Just the two of us. I left her in the kitchen crying into her cup of tea, whimpering, 'I'm just so proud of you,' over and over again. If she carries on like this, it's not going to be a great day out.

I've been on a high ever since the best day out I've had in ages. That set me up for the week and things have just got better and better. I think it has been the best week of my life, and that's no exaggeration.

I haven't told anyone, not even Frankie, but I had my driving test yesterday and I only went and freaking passed. First time. I am still buzzing.

Mum told me this morning she sorted out the insurance so I could drive her car. 'I've been forced to sell a kidney, so don't you dare hit anything or we'll have to sell the house and live in a tent,' she said as she put the phone down. I didn't dare ask how much it cost. Luckily, we moved on from that conversation quickly.

Reggie lets us know that the post is about to arrive in his usual way. He knows the sound of the van and starts barking before the postie gets out of the car. Then, once the letters have been delivered and the postie walks back down the drive, Reggie looks at us both as if to say 'You're welcome, once again I have saved your lives from the postie of doom.'

I run downstairs in case there's anything for me. Collecting the letters, Mum looks at me with excitement. 'Dani, there's something for you.'

'I can't have my license back already,' I say, as that's the only thing on my mind – that little card of freedom with a picture that isn't great, but I don't care. It will mean I can drive, and I don't care what I look like, as long as I am behind the wheel.

'Wait, I need to be sitting down for this,' she says. She hands me the envelope and my heart starts to beat faster and a wave of nervous excitement washes over me. 'Open it, for crying out loud,' Mum squeals, sending Reggie racing to the window to double-check the postie has been dealt with and doesn't need to be told to go away again.

I open it. 'Shit,' I whisper, staring at the letter, not knowing what else to say. My head is spinning as I realise that I am going to need to work hard, and that my future has opened up before my eyes.

'It's okay, don't worry, love, you can apply again next year.' Mum stands up to give me a hug and as she does, sees what is written on the letter.

'Shit.' It takes a split second for her to start crying. 'You did it. You did it, Dani.'

I have been offered a provisional place at both the local Uni and the Uni that Jane wants me to go to. I have choices. Well, I have to get the grades, but as long as I get the grades, I can go to Uni. I have provisional places at another two universities too, but seeing all of the options available to me, I know it's a question of location more than anything else.

'You know, whatever you want to do and wherever you want to go, I'll support you,' Mum says, still crying.

'I need to get the grades, then I can worry about where I go,' I say as the reality of the situation begins to sink in.

'You will. You can do anything you put your mind to. You've proven that time and time again, but this week, you've excelled yourself.'

'I really have, so can I drive us into town?' I think the time is right to ask, as Mum won't be able to say 'no' to me today.

'Dani, you can definitely drive us into town.'

I'm right; she isn't able to say 'no' today! I won't push my luck though because she might start talking about the cost of insurance and selling her body parts again.

'I got my Uni stuff back x,' I send to Frankie, wondering if she has heard too. I know she is training until lunchtime and want to talk to her face-to-face, not just tell her the good news in a message, but I'm too excited to hold it in. When I text her about the offers and then add in about how I've also passed my driving test, I think she's disappointed I hadn't told her it was going to happen, so I send another message: 'Fancy pizza later? x.' I know that she will forgive anything for her favourite food.

Forty

That's it now. No more messing about. I'm going to ride this wave of good stuff that's happening and get the grades I need to go to Uni.

I've had way too much fun celebrating and have managed to forget the deadlines that are looming.

It isn't just me who has enjoyed good news about the future. When I was in town with mum, my phone was going off every two seconds.

'I'm in, I'm going to Uni! x.'

'Shit. Post, I need to get up x.'

'Did you get in? x.'

'I'm not dressed. I need to find my pants before I can check the post x.'

Katie was up early waiting for the post every day this week, but in my excitement about my driving test, I had totally forgotten that we were waiting for the letters. Maya didn't forget, but her lie-in on a Saturday couldn't be interrupted by the small matter of her future career.

'I'm IN. I'm IN! x.'

That was three out of four of us. We were waiting for Frankie who joined in the excitement and asked me if I wanted to invite everyone for pizza.

Callie who declared after I texted everyone – 'Uni is for losers, but pizza is for winners, see ya laterz x' – had decided a long time ago that she was going to go straight into an apprenticeship. She had a job lined up with a tattoo artist and would be earning good money while we were getting into stupid amounts of debt. I did wonder if I was doing the right thing, but at that moment, was too excited to think about the debt.

Now that the celebrations are over, there's no getting around the fact that the choices will only remain available if I get the grades they have asked for. They're doable, I hope, but it won't be easy. That's the point, I suppose!

I'm getting myself focused. I don't just need to get the grades; I want to get the grades. I have never felt this motivated before, so I think I should make the most of it.

Goals

- It is May and I have my black tag. Training has to stay high up on my priority list, as without it, I get lazy and feel crap. So, I will go to every training session, practice at home and I will get my black tag.
- It's Easter and I am up to date with all of my Sixth Form work. Not long now until the Easter break and I have so much to do I could cry. I have my daily plan and all I need to do now is follow it and not get behind.
- It is August and I have the grades I need to go to Uni. I don't need to worry about which Uni, I just need to get the grades to the choice will be mine, and not theirs.

Success

- I can drive! I can legally drive! That's the biggest success of my life so far. Passing first time is a bonus too as Mum says I now have bragging rights for life. It's weird but a few people have asked me if I passed first time and it feels really good to nod, saying 'of course'.
- Getting the provisional places at the universities is an awesome feeling. Not just because I can now work towards a career I'll hopefully enjoy, but I feel valued. The Uni people have read my application and feel I have something to offer, that's pretty cool.

Gratitude

- Time with my friends. This has helped me a lot, in ways that they'll never know. Being able to share it with Frankie has made it extra special and I think it has brought us closer.

- Jane helping with my Uni application. I know that she made it so much better by rewriting it for me. She has told me how proud she is of me and that means a lot.
- Mum saying that she will support whatever I decide about Uni. That has taken the pressure off me as I wasn't sure if she'd push me to move away. I still think that she would like Sammy to move in, but I don't know if that will happen while I'm still at home. It's nice to know I can stay if I want to.
- Right now, I'm just grateful to be enjoying life so much, to have awesome people around me, and to be able to see a great future opening up for me. It's exciting.

Forty-One

'Jesus, Dani, what did you do that for?' Mum screamed this morning when she saw me leaning over the sink, getting paler by the second with blood pouring out of my finger.

'It's not like I did it on purpose. It really hurts.' I was willing myself not to cry, or be sick. I wanted to do both but couldn't get my legs to move away from the sink.

'We're going to have to get you to A & E, just let me phone work.'

I thought Mum was phoning for an ambulance but no, never mind me losing a river of blood down the sink, she needed to postpone her meeting. 'Mum, I feel quite ill,' I said. I must have looked quite ill as she put the phone down and grabbed a tea towel. Wrapping it around my hand she asked me to hold it tight while she fetched her keys, then helped me out to the car.

'Please don't bleed on the car seat.'

'Seriously? You're thinking about your meeting and your car when I could be dying here.' As I said the words I knew that I was exaggerating a little bit, but it really hurt and there was a lot of blood.

'You've cut your finger, Dani. I don't think it's life threatening. Bleeding on the car seat could be life threatening though, I love this car.'

It felt like my finger was about to come away from my hand, but I wasn't going to argue about the definition of a 'cut'. My focus was on holding the tea towel around my finger and doing my very best not to be sick. I was sure that being sick in the car would be life threatening too.

The really annoying thing was that I had been trying to be helpful. Being helpful was bad for my health. I had made tuna sandwiches for lunch and Mum had always lectured me on washing the tin for the recycling.

Her words to me this morning had been, 'You need to make sure it's clean, especially so that Reggie doesn't lick it and cut himself.' Oh, the irony.

I'd been washing up the tin and without thinking, had swept my hand around the inside of it. Then I saw the water had turned red followed by a searing rush of pain and, lifting my hand of out the washing up bowl, saw the skin of my index finger falling away from where it should have been.

The nurse I saw in A & E was much more sympathetic than Mum had been. 'Don't worry, we'll clean that up,' he told me as I bled on the floor of the triage room. 'I'm going to have to clean that up which won't be comfortable and then we'll stitch you up.'

'Will it take long?' Mum asked.

'We'll have you out of here in no time,' he said to me. 'Can I interest you in a drink and a sandwich? Tuna?'

The look on my face said it all.

'Too soon? How about cheese?'

My appetite never stayed away for long and after a drink and something to eat I started to feel better, but my finger was throbbing. The nurse talked to me while he cleaned it up but I couldn't reply to what he was saying, I was mumbling, 'That hurts, that hurts a lot, that really hurts,' on a loop. He ignored me and carried on talking.

'All done,' he announced.

I looked down and saw the world's smallest bandage around my finger. 'What about the stitches?' I asked.

'It wasn't as bad as it looked, I used Steri-Strips so you'll just need to make an appointment to see the nurse at your GP's surgery in a week or so and they'll check it over for you.'

'I don't know whether to be happy, or be embarrassed. Is that really it?' I couldn't believe that after all that blood, I essentially had a plaster on my finger.

'Is that it?' Mum repeated as she came back in to take me

home. She had made her excuses as soon as the tea towel had been removed. 'That's a relief.'

Thanking the nurse and rushing me back to the car, Mum was wittering on about dropping me off at home and that I'd have to walk to Sixth Form.

'Don't I get the day off to recover from the trauma?' I asked, thinking it was worth a try.

'There's nothing wrong with your legs or your ears. You can walk to Sixth Form and you can listen.'

She used the 'Mum voice' that I knew not to argue with. 'Do you think I'll be able to train?' I asked, and immediately regretted it.

'So, you can go to taekwondo but you can't sit in a classroom?'

Yeah, I knew that was a mistake. I kept my mouth shut for the rest of the journey and decided that I would go to Sixth Form, even if it was just to share my near-death experience with my friends and try to get some sympathy.

'That's the world's shittiest war wound,' Frankie said when I arrived at college. She laughed at my bandage questioning whether I really had needed to go to A & E.

'What does it take to get some sympathy around here?' I whimpered.

'More than a plaster,' said Maya. 'I mean, maybe if you had real stitches, or a sling, or a plaster cast we could sign. Not that though, you don't get any sympathy for that.'

I gave up. My attention shifted to the fact I might actually not be able to train. It was amazing how motivated I became when I was not able to do something. I'd missed training for loads of stupid reasons, but as soon as I had a genuine reason for not being able to use my hand, I could come up with twenty solutions and ways to make it happen. What was that about?

Funnily enough, the same thing didn't happen when it came to finding a way to take notes. 'I can take a photo of yours, can't

I?' I pleaded, dropping my pen for dramatic effect.

'Sure, but only this week.' Frankie smiled. 'And when I get a paper cut from scribbling your notes, I want sympathy too.'

'Deal.'

Forty-Two

'Are you kidding me?' Frankie said earlier, a little bit too seriously for my liking.

I wasn't sure if she was joking so laughed to lighten the mood and replied, 'But this way we'll get to see more of each other. If you're free too, obviously.' I realised I had made an assumption that Frankie would work around my new colour-coded schedule.

I thought it was a brilliant idea. I wanted to do everything in my power to pass the exams, pass my grading and see Frankie and my friends.

'You have actually scheduled me. I have been colour-coded and scheduled.'

I still couldn't tell if she was messing around. 'You're green, because it's the colour of your favourite running shoes,' I said, but that didn't help.

She examined my schedule, trying to figure out when our allocated time together would be. 'Hold on.' I knew what she had spotted. I was going to ask her about it later on, but it looked like we were going to have the conversation now. 'This is a green weekend. Well, a Saturday evening and Sunday morning?'

'Mum and Sammy are going away. One of Sammy's friends is getting married. I thought you might want to come over. You know, stay over. If you want. I know you might be busy.' I was rambling. I felt silly, she was holding my schedule and it was the most unromantic way I could have thought of to ask her to stay over.

'I'd love to,' she replied. 'Maybe I can get on board with the whole schedule thing.' She kissed me. 'Reggie will be staying downstairs, won't he?'

'I think he'll be okay with that,' I said, pretty sure he wouldn't be okay with that. More importantly, I was okay with that. 'It's a date then.'

The moment was shattered by the man himself bouncing into my room and making himself comfortable at the foot of my bed.

'See what I mean?' Frankie joked, while picking up his favourite toy and winding him up with it.

'If you weren't so much fun, he wouldn't want to spend so much time with you,' I told her. She couldn't be grumpy with us when we were complimenting her. 'Now, piss off because green time has ended and it is now red time.'

I knew that Frankie had to go to a running club thing anyway, and it wasn't like I would rather do my Psychology essay than spend time with her. I was impressed that I had almost made it through the first day of my schedule though, and I was on target.

With a final throw of Reggie's favourite toy, Frankie got up to leave, creating a pathway of destruction thanks to her rubbish aim.

'I hope you've got a colour code for tidying up Reggie's mess,' she said as she headed for the door.

'His colour is brown, you can guess why.' I laughed. I knew she would think it was poo bag related, but he was actually brown because it was the colour of his favourite toy. I followed Frankie downstairs.

'I'm such a loser,' I said to Reggie, after waving goodbye to Frankie. 'I don't care though, you love me, don't you?'

Wagging his tail and dropping his toy at my feet I whispered, 'I'll take that as a yes.'

I was nervous and excited that I had asked Frankie about staying over. We both knew what that meant and I was relieved she was so relaxed about it. That had helped me feel less pressured, but my head was already overthinking everything.

'Schedule, just stick to the schedule or you won't get anything done,' I told myself, heading for the kitchen and not back my room.

'Who are you talking to?'

'Mum, you made me jump,' I shouted. 'I didn't hear you

come home.'

'Is Frankie here?' she asked. 'Or are you having a deep and meaningful conversation with Reggie?'

'I was talking to myself,' I admitted. 'I'm trying to talk myself into writing an essay.'

'I'll make tea and bring you a snack to help you while you're writing. We don't want you having another kitchen related accident, do we?'

That was a result. I hadn't factored in the extra time it would take for me to type while my hand was sore and swollen though. It was annoying that it hurt so much and I only had a little plaster and a swollen bruise to show for it. Sitting at my desk and typing with one hand made essay writing even less fun than usual. I didn't think that was possible.

Forty-Three

That was the most amazing weekend.

After winding myself up into what I can only describe now as panic, I almost cancelled. I wrote messages saying I was feeling poorly, saying I was sick and even one saying that I needed to take Reggie to the vet. I deleted that one as quickly as possible as Mum would say I was tempting fate.

The thing is, I did feel sick! My head was spinning and I had questions going over and over in my mind. 'Do I feel like this because it's not what I want?' 'Do I feel like this because I don't want to be with Frankie?' 'Am I ready for this?'

'If in doubt, don't.' These were always Jane's words of wisdom when I questioned my actions. She would follow that up with a lecture about not avoiding things I really did want to do, so I was never really sure whether to take her advice or not.

In the end I looked at my phone, ready to send a message to tell Frankie I wasn't feeling well when her name popped up on the screen. 'Can't wait 2 c u, got pizza and ur fave film x.'

In a heartbeat, the pressure went away again. I really wanted to see her and knew that we could just chill out and see what happened. Maybe it was that simple.

It was that simple.

Waking up with Frankie was the most incredible start to the day. I was worried that I would feel awkward or embarrassed, that something might have changed or that being close to someone would bring back feelings that I never wanted to experience again.

That couldn't be further from the reality.

Right now, I feel like the luckiest girl on the planet.

Forty-Four

'Believe me, I don't want to go either,' I said to Frankie earlier today while I was packing to go to Jane's for a couple of days.

'You'll have a lot more fun if you stay here with me.'

'I know that. That's why I don't want to go!' I admitted, knowing that she was right, but that I would also be setting myself up to fail my exams as there was no way I'd choose revision over seeing her at that moment. 'It's not for long, and I'd have more time if I didn't have to go and get this stupid hand checked over first.'

Frankie was only supposed to be staying for a few minutes on her way to training, but an hour had passed and Mum was getting grumpy.

'We're going to be late, Dani. Have you packed your bag?' She was going to have a break with Sammy once she'd abandoned me at Jane's and didn't want to be held up by the GP appointment either. While they were off to the Lakes with my dog, I was being sent to Jane's for a final pre-exam boot camp. I had done my best to convince them all that Reggie wanted to come with me, but even he hadn't look convinced that boot camp at Jane's would be more fun than walking the hills with Mum. He had a point!

'That's my cue to leave,' Frankie said as she raced to the door.

'You're coming for dinner next weekend, aren't you Frankie?' Mum shouted before she could escape. 'Jane's looking forward to meeting you.'

'*Would* miss it for the world, Mrs M, enjoy your holiday.' Frankie winked at us and left.

I knew she was nervous about meeting Jane. When I'd invited her to join us all for dinner her first response had been, 'That's going to be scarier than meeting your mum.'

'You met my mum ages ago,' I'd said, a bit confused.

'Yeah, but it's different now. This is like an official meet the girlfriend thing. What if she doesn't like me, or can read my mind and she tells you what I'm thinking.'

'I know what you'll be thinking.' I'd laughed. 'You'll be deciding between pizza or burger and chips on the menu.'

'Fair point.'

I was pretty sure that Jane would like Frankie. There was nothing not to like, but I supposed I was biased.

Mum jerked me back from my daydream. She had a magical way of killing them. 'Seriously, Dani. GET IN THE CAR!'

Mum spent most of the appointment at the GP's checking her watch while the nurse was trying to explain to us both that my hand had healed well but there would be a small scar.

'I'm listening,' I said. 'Don't worry. Mum's not bothered about a scar and I'll make up a cool story about how it happened.' I felt a little bit embarrassed by Mum's behaviour and wondered when I'd turned into the parent.

'You were really rude,' I said as we left.

'We're late. You need to get to Jane's and I need to go and enjoy myself.'

'Sounds like you're all set for enjoying yourself,' I whispered, knowing that now was not the time to make any jokes.

'Sorry,' she said. 'I just need to have a couple of days away from work and I don't mean to take it out on you.'

I forgot that Mum had her own stuff going on. I had no idea what was happening at her work, and I wasn't sure I'd understand if she told me.

'You'll be able to forget all about it with your two favourite men,' I said. 'And I hear there's a lot of sheep shit for Reggie to enjoy in the Lakes, so you'll be kept busy. Did you pack his wet wipes?'

'I bought extra,' she said, finally looking a bit more relaxed.

The second that Mum had closed Jane's front door, I heard the words, 'You had a good weekend with Frankie then?'

How does she do it? How does she know everything?

'Yeah, it was good, thanks,' I said, desperately trying to sound relaxed while my face turned the colour of a post box.

'I'll be having the "hurt her and I'll hurt you" chat with her at the weekend, I think,' Jane teased.

'Don't you dare. Anyway, you'd need Lucy's help to kick her arse, not that you'd be able to catch her, she's a runner.'

'I'll think of something. As long as she doesn't hurt you, I won't need to ask Lucy to kick her arse.' She softened and smiled at me as she added, 'I'm so glad you're happy.'

I am happy. Last time I was at Jane's, I was relieved that I had some time to escape the pressure of getting closer to Frankie. This time, I'd give anything to be with her. The pressure was only in my head, it was a combination of fear and of not trusting my gut. If I had relaxed and let myself think things through rationally rather than panicking and overthinking it all, I'd have saved myself a lot of headaches.

Maybe I should relax and go with the flow more often. I've been told a few times that I need to learn to trust my gut feeling and my instincts. What's the worst that can happen if I'm honest with myself? If the weekend with Frankie taught me anything, it's that going with the flow can be a lot more fun than overthinking!

'Missing you x,' I send to Frankie.

'Right bak attcha x,' she replies.

Forty-Five

I think I needed the break at Jane's. It wasn't until I had my first lie-in in weeks that I realised how tired I was. It wasn't just feeling like crap that had drained my energy, feeling great had been quite overwhelming too. It wasn't a bad thing, but Jane explained that it was easy to forget that you still need to rest, even when you were feeling brilliant.

'It's like a rollercoaster, Dani,' she said, knowing that I loved a superfast rollercoaster and she hated them. 'If we were both sitting at the top of the big dipper, waiting for it to drop at lightning speed, how would you feel?'

I could feel my body responding as I thought about it. 'I'd be excited, my heart would be racing, I'd be sweating and my stomach would be doing somersaults.' I was feeling these things as I replied. I was talking faster and more animated, wishing there was a rollercoaster nearby.

'Now tell me how I'd be feeling,' she asked, looking paler by the second so must have been thinking about being on the ultimate rollercoaster.

'You'd be literally shitting yourself.' I laughed, knowing that was probably true. 'You'd be feeling sick, you'd be sweating, your heart would probably be racing, you'd be desperate to get off.'

'So, we're actually feeling the same, but what you're calling excitement is what I'm calling fear.'

Jane gave me a minute to think about that. 'So, what does that mean?' I asked, wondering if I was being stupid.

'It's just chemicals, Dani. Our bodies are being flooded with the same chemicals, but in that situation, you love it and I hate it.' She went quiet again, and I was starting to understand what she meant. 'When we get down from that rollercoaster, we'll both struggle to talk for a minute or two, we'll both have quite intense feelings of either how awesome it was or relief that it's over and we'll both feel quite tired later on.'

I could see where she was going with it; there was always a hidden message when it came to Jane's mini-lectures.

'Your life has been a rollercoaster.'

There it was – the not-so-hidden message.

'At the moment, you're on a high and it's amazing to see. I want this high to last a lifetime for you, but you still need to rest, to let your mind and body process what's happening.'

'I did need a good night's sleep,' I admitted. 'I feel a bit better already. I think I've been buzzing for a while, like I'm on a high because things are going so well.'

'That's brilliant, and if anyone deserves to be enjoying a buzz, it's you. All I'm saying is that it's more likely to last and you're more likely to enjoy it, if you also give yourself a break every so often.'

After the last few weeks, I definitely needed time out. For once, things were going well, I mean, really well. Jane had taken some time off work, so along with making sure I spent time revising, we had a really good time together. She took me out for lunch, we went out with Lucy and she took me to see one of her favourite local bands.

Sitting in the pub, having watched her enjoy the band and having enjoyed it myself, although I might not admit to that again, I felt like things had changed. I felt like I was sitting with a friend, not sitting with Mum's friend who had been tasked with helping me, looking after me or fixing me. I hoped that she'd noticed the shift too, I hoped that she'd enjoyed the time we'd had together as much as I had.

That feeling continued on the way back home to my house when Jane asked about Frankie. She wanted to know more about her and if there was anything she shouldn't say over dinner.

'I can't think of anything. She's pretty relaxed. Just don't freak her out with weird questions that make it sound like you're analysing her.'

'Now you're just spoiling my fun,' Jane said. 'You know I'm going to have to freak her out a little bit.'

'Sure, I'd expect nothing less,' I agreed, knowing that Frankie could give as good as she got. It would be a fun evening.

It was. It was much more fun that I thought it would be.

'I wish my folks were this cool,' Frankie said as Mum and Jane went to get us some drinks.

'My folks?' I said, wondering what she meant.

'Well, yeah. The way you talk about Jane, she's like the mum everyone wants, isn't she? She can get you to work hard and teaches you what life is all about, while also being your best mate and having a laugh with you. You got a cool Mum AND Jane, that's pretty lucky.'

I had to agree. 'Right now, I do feel really lucky, and it's not just because of my folks,' I said, squeezing Frankie's hand and wanting to kiss her.

'Cheers,' said Mum, sitting down next to Frankie, as if to protect her from an onslaught of questions.

Jane excused herself. 'You know what I want to order,' she said, heading for the ladies.

The waiter appeared and as Mum had almost finished ordering Jane's food, he asked, 'Would your partner like chips or salad with that.'

Frankie and I stared at each other, then at Mum, desperately trying not to laugh.

Without skipping a beat, Mum simply replied, 'She'd like salad, please.'

At that moment, Jane returned to find us all in tears. 'What did I miss?'

'Mrs M was just outed by the waiter,' Frankie eventually

managed to say, setting us all off again.

'I just didn't want to be the odd one out.' Mum joined in.

'Well, babe, you're one of the cool kids now,' Jane declared. 'Cheers to that.'

I had to pinch myself to be sure that I wasn't dreaming. What was probably totally normal to most people, felt like a dream come true for me. I never thought I could feel so happy, genuinely happy, ever again. I knew it was just a meal out, I knew that everyone had their good times and their bad times, but for me, it was a big deal to be feeling like this and I wanted to enjoy it forever.

Forty-Six

Of all the ways my brain could choose to make me feel like crap, I wasn't ready for this one. I had the weirdest dream and when I woke up it took me a while to convince myself that it wasn't real. It certainly felt real. When I woke up my heart was racing, I couldn't breathe properly and I was panicking, actually panicking.

I haven't had a dream like that for ages. It had happened all the time after the rape, I would be too scared to sleep and would desperately try to stay awake, but my body would win the battle. This time, I dreamt that the man who attacked me was chasing me. I'm not sure where we were, I didn't recognise the place, but I was running as fast as I could down a quiet road. There were cars driving past and I caught the eyes of the drivers who looked away and didn't stop. I came to a high fence, the same sort of mesh wiring that surrounds tennis courts. I looked back and I could see he was still running towards me, then I woke up.

I felt as if I had been running for hours. My body ached and I was exhausted. I was too frightened to close my eyes again so I went downstairs and made a drink, making sure that Reggie knew he could go up to my room. I needed to feel safe and even though by then I had been able to talk myself around to the fact it was only a dream, my body still responded as if it had been real.

'What made my brain do that to me?' I now ask Reggie, who responds in the only way he knows how, with a head tilt and the offer of a paw.

As soon as I ask the question I know the answer. Mum told me about a crime drama on television that I needed to avoid. She's good at checking the programmes out for me. It's annoying as I love crime dramas but it seems that if they don't include in the story that someone has been raped or sexually abused it's just not 'dramatic' enough.

I happily avoided that programme. It's not like I watch much TV anyway so didn't give it another thought until yesterday evening. Maybe the people who spend so long creating real-life dramas that someone like me can choose to avoid with a bit of warning, should also think about the bloody adverts that pop up when I'm having a half-hour break from revision and trying to enjoy my dinner.

Seriously, the advert left very little to the imagination, but just enough to make sure my brain went into a little panic. I thought I let it go quite quickly, and turned off the TV, put on some music and finished my dinner. The lyrics were flooding my brain and the volume meant that nothing else could infiltrate my system, or so I thought.

'Is this a sign that things are going to go wrong again?' I ask Reggie, but he has gone back to sleep and is snoring at the foot of my bed.

The dream is a reminder that my brain might never fully recover from what happened. Even though things have been amazing and I've been really happy, it doesn't take much for my brain to respond as if I am back in a life or death situation. I know that it is trying to keep me safe in its own primitive way, but it's very annoying.

The more I fight it, the worse it becomes. If I try to stay awake after a dream like that, my body takes over and makes me extra tired. If I try to go back to sleep, my brain starts thinking about things that mean I can't even close my eyes. What's that about?

I'm supposed to be seeing Frankie but know that I will be grumpy and probably snap at her. When I felt like this before, I was on edge for hours afterwards, like my body was on some sort of comedown.

'Really soz, got a mad headache, see u tomo x,' I send, hoping that will be enough to not only mean that I can stay in bed and sort myself out, but that she also won't message me too much. I know that sounds really horrible, but I don't have much control over what I say when I feel like this, and I don't want to be a bitch.

'Revision, tomo at mine, be there! x,' she replies.

That gives me twenty-four hours. That's enough, as long as I can get some decent sleep and not endure another dream marathon at world record pace.

The one thing that makes me want to close my eyes and go to sleep is revision. That's what I am supposed to be doing today anyway. A few pages of the psychology book and I'll probably be sound asleep and only dreaming of social learning theory. Even writing those three words has made me sleepy!

Forty-Seven

I was right, there's nothing like some psychology revision to numb my brain. I guess this means I'll be doing quite a lot of sleeping when I'm at Uni.

It took less than a chapter to send me back to sleep yesterday and after a couple of hours I woke up to find that I had been using the book as a pillow. It wasn't very comfortable but I hoped it meant that I had absorbed the information while I was sleeping. Reggie had been replaced with a note from Mum.

'I've taken Reggie for his walk, any idea how he found his way to your room when the kitchen door was left closed last night? Get some revision done x.'

That was about as subtle as Mum ever got, but it was Mum-speak for 'don't let Reggie upstairs, you know the rules'.

I was quite productive, once I got going, and felt better by lunchtime. With an evening of training ticked off and after my good night's sleep last night, thankfully without any running, I was all set for a revision session at Frankie's.

Yeah, like that was going to happen.

I did at least show willing. I took my rucksack full of books and my schedule. I had optimistically drawn a plan for the day, given each subject an allocated focus, and had scheduled a decent lunch break.

'Let's see the schedule, you geek,' Frankie joked when I got to her house and we'd settled down to work. She reached for her pens.

'Don't mess it up,' I said, handing her the carefully thought through revision plan.

'I won't mess it up, but I will make it much more fun.' She scribbled hearts all over the page, kissed me and said, 'There, I've still left an hour for lunch, now tell me you'd rather revise?'

No contest. After absolutely no revision at all, but the most amazing day, it took all the self-control I could find to get up and get ready to go home.

'Mum will be home soon, so you should at least get dressed,' Frankie said as I was packing up the books that hadn't been opened.

'Yeah, I'm not sure this counts as a study day and didn't you promise her that's what you'd be doing?

She looked at me in a way that made me melt, saying, 'I've certainly learnt something new.'

'Shut up.' I said, pulling on my jeans and feeling embarrassed.

'I've had an amazing time, there's no way I'll be able to concentrate on revision this evening.'

I'd forgotten that despite calling this a study day, we hadn't actually studied so I was going to have to motivate myself later on too.

'How about you come over for dinner tomorrow evening?' Frankie asked. 'You know, like a proper dinner and meet my folks.'

'I've met your folks loads of times,' I said, wondering what she meant.

'Yeah, but not properly, not as my girlfriend.'

That word made me feel weird. Not in a bad way, just in an unfamiliar way. I was somebody's girlfriend. That was pretty cool. 'That sounds good, thank you.'

'All cool, I'll text you when I've checked with Mum about what time and all that. Now piss off and stop distracting me, I have work to do.'

Walking home, I wondered how I would be able to concentrate all evening.

So at least I've been struggling to concentrate for good reasons. No, better than that – amazing reasons. Maybe it doesn't matter whether I feel on top of the world or in the depths of despair, revision is still the solution for numbing my brain!

I am starting to worry that I am behind on revision. The last couple of days have shattered my schedule and regardless of the fact I wouldn't have changed today for anything, I still need to pass the exams.

I need to prioritise again, especially as I have everything going to happen all at once: handing in the last pieces of coursework, the dreaded exams and my next grading.

Goals

- It is May and I have my black tag. Well, that's next week! I have been doing okay, I'm nearly there I think but this is a big deal and I want it to be perfect.
- It's the last day of formal lessons and I have handed in all of my coursework. I definitely need to get on this case if that's going to happen. I'm two days behind, and that's not good at all. One piece of coursework is being submitted for the second time because I wasn't happy with the low mark, so I need to make that a lot better.

Success

- Not spending a week in bed after the horrible dream. I think I'm learning to deal with things much better.
- Not freaking out at all during my day with Frankie. That might sound stupid, but being able to trust her and enjoy being with her is a big deal for me.

Gratitude

- Frankie, Frankie and Frankie! She's so good to me, I do feel so grateful that she wants to be with me.
- Reggie being my safety dog when I needed him, even though he fell asleep! That night, it wasn't enough that he was in the house, I needed him to be closer to me. He understood.

So, the question now is do I need to spend an hour re-writing my schedule, or do I just try to catch up? It's probably unrealistic to think I can do two days' work in one evening, so I'll give myself the time to plan, and then celebrate by sticking to the plan. All I really need to do this evening is that one essay. If I can make that amazing, then I can sort out revision afterwards.

Forty-Eight

'I can't believe you actually finished it,' Frankie squealed when I showed her the essay. 'I couldn't get my head together to study at all after our day together, so I went for a run and crashed out.'

I felt even more proud of myself that I had managed to motivate myself to get the essay finished.

'It's actually pretty good,' she told me. 'Maybe I'm a good influence on you after all?'

'It's a shame I can't say the same thing back,' I replied, feeling bad that Frankie was even more behind in her work than I was, but knowing I couldn't do it for her.

'I'll find my superpower as the deadlines get closer,' she joked. 'You know me, I work better under pressure.'

'Let's hope that's true,' said a voice from the kitchen. 'Hello, Dani, it's good to see you, especially with a completed essay.'

'Thanks for inviting me,' I called back to Dani's mum. 'I probably should admit that it's the second time I've written that essay as it was pretty poor the first time.'

'As long as you've learnt from the mistake and you get the grade in the end, it doesn't matter.'

Frankie rolled her eyes. 'She never says that to me.'

Dinner with Frankie's folks involved a lot less laughter than dinner with Mum and Jane, but it felt much more grown up. Her parents discussed their days at work and asked us about ours. They talked about politics, which I didn't really understand, but saw Frankie in a completely different light as she joined in, saying, 'I think his left-wing approach will help the Country in the long run.'

What did that even mean? I didn't really care, but I was impressed. Her parents seemed to understand what she was talking about and the conversation developed without me. I enjoyed listening, without any pressure, and seeing how different Frankie's family was to my own. Mum always told me about her day, but it was more about the bitch in the office who stole the last drop of milk from the communal fridge, or the fact her manager was working from home for the third time that week and incapable of answering emails. I didn't think I'd ever heard Mum talking about politics. I bet Sammy talked about politics, so if the two families ever got together for dinner, he'd enjoy himself.

What was I thinking? Was I already planning my future with Frankie? Family dinners and grown up conversations; I'd even just invited Sammy! What was going on in my head?

'Dani? Dani are you okay?' I heard through the mist of seeing my future flash before my eyes.

'Sorry, I'm just really enjoying the food,' I said, unsure about how much of the conversation I had missed.

'Well recovered.' Frankie winked at me, knowing that having a finished essay meant I could do no wrong in her mum's eyes this evening.

'Frankie tells me that you have some wonderful university offers available to you. Have you decided where you're going to go?'

Everything I'd been thinking about since September merged in a knot in my stomach and travelled to my throat, where it stayed, preventing me from speaking. I smiled, praying that words would form and managed, 'I think the results will decide for me, but it's exciting to have the choices.'

Happy with that response, Frankie's mum agreed and started talking about her university days. Luckily, she didn't probe any further as I didn't know what to say. I suddenly felt incredibly stupid that the real reason I didn't have a clue about where I wanted to go was because I didn't know if I could leave my dog.

I knew that I couldn't say that out loud, not to Frankie's family anyway. It was bad enough that Jane didn't understand when we first talked about it, so there was no way I was going to talk about it with anyone else.

I couldn't shake the feeling though, wondering if the answer would magically appear one day and I would be certain about what I wanted to do. I hoped so, but I wasn't convinced.

Nodding in all of the right places, I thought I'd got away with not listening to Frankie's mum's tales of university life. It wasn't that I wasn't interested, it was just the thought of living in halls and starting from scratch in a new place, all by myself, was terrifying. Frankie found it exciting. She called it 'a whole new adventure' and I thought that was awesome. I just didn't feel the same.

'Only a little piece for me,' I requested as the homemade dessert appeared.

'What's wrong with you? This is the taste of heaven,' Frankie's dad said, quickly followed by, 'I'll have Dani's extra share, that's no problem at all.'

'I have to practice for my grading when I get I home,' I told them. 'Dessert looks amazing, but it will make me want to just lie on the sofa.'

'Sounds like a perfect plan to me.' Frankie's dad chucked, tucking in to his second helping.

'Good for you, Dani. Ignore him. He doesn't need an excuse to lie on the sofa. What is the grading for? Frankie said you like to fight?'

I looked at Frankie, wondering exactly what she had told her mum.

'Don't worry, I said that you like to fight in a nice way,' she said.

'Something like that,' I told her mum. 'I'm training to get my black belt in Taekwondo and tomorrow I have my grading for my black tag, which is the belt before the full black.'

Lowering her spoon and looking at Frankie, she said, 'Why didn't you tell me Dani was so accomplished. She's an elite sportswoman, has passed her driving test first time and finishes her essays.'

'That might be why I didn't tell you,' Frankie said, and we felt a speech coming on.

Luckily, Frankie's mum kept it short and I did feel humbled by the fact she seemed impressed by what I was doing. It was easy to forget what you'd done when you were always striving to complete the next thing on the list.

'Please let me know how you get on tomorrow,' Frankie's mum said as I was putting my coat on to leave. 'I really hope you get your tag as then you're in touching distance of your dream.'

I smiled at her excitement, thanked her for dinner and felt as if I had been given a much-needed injection of enthusiasm. My dream of wearing that black belt really was in touching distance.

Forty-Nine

The only thing that put a dampener on my mood after my grading was the reply I had from Frankie to my text. It didn't last long, but for a few minutes, she burst the bubble.

'Check out the pic x,' I sent, along with a photo of me, being handed my new belt by my instructor, the most patient man on the planet.

It had made it all the more special when he'd presented the belt as he had been such an integral part of the achievement. Not wanting to let him down had always been part of my motivation to train. Frankie knew this, so I thought she'd understand what it meant to me.

'One more reason 4 Mum 2 think ur the daughter she wished she had. x,' she replied.

I didn't know if she was joking, but I didn't care. Would it have killed her to say 'congratulations'? I chose not to reply. I wouldn't have said anything that would have made either of us feel better, so I deleted her message and sent the message to everyone else.

'Wowzers, that's so cool,' Katie replied. 'Will you kick Cal's ass for me, he's being a knob again x.'

'You're so nearly a pro, congrats x,' Maya replied.

Callie won the prize for the best reply though. She sent me a picture. It was a graffiti style drawing of me doing a high kick, wearing my black belt, with the message, 'I'm working on ur first tattoo, so hurry up and get the black one. x.'

That picture quickly became my screen saver. I loved my friends! They knew exactly what to say even if Frankie was caught up in her own stuff.

Mum appeared. 'You need a shower before we go and celebrate,' she gushed as she hugged me. 'You did it. You have your black tag, it's just incredible.'

She left me to tell my instructor how wonderful he was, as she did after every grading, so I began to pack my bag to go home. Taking a moment, I sat on the bench in the changing room, holding the belt in my hands.

I had done it. My eyes were about to leak and I looked up to find one of the younger kids looking at the belt too.

'Can I hold it? I'll be careful, I promise,' she asked, reaching for the belt.

She held it as if it was the most delicate item on earth. 'I want to be as good as you,' she said, handing it back. 'Congratulations, you're amazing.'

'Thank you, I really appreciate that,' I told her, and meant every word. I knew that she'd be one of the group I'd be helping in the coming weeks, so I would be able to work with her to get her first belt. It wouldn't be long before she was sitting on the bench with her black belt. The time had flown by since I was in her position, looking in awe at the people with their different coloured belts. What was I talking about? I still looked at them all in awe. It would take me a while until I remembered that I was now one of them, a part of the club and someone who had worked her way through the ranks.

Hearing a beep, I reached for my phone. 'Soz, babe. That came out all wrong. I'm so proud of you. x.'

That was better! Feeling instantly rejuvenated, I replied, 'It's all cool. Going out to eat and will need to sleep for a week. x.'

I didn't have time to sleep for a week though. After the exhilaration of passing my grading, came the trepidation of the final day of lessons.

Don't get me wrong, it wasn't like I wanted to keep going to lessons forever, but I definitely didn't want the exams to start.

The day was a weird mix of emotions. We were all knackered after lots of late nights getting the essays finished while being energised at the thought of never having to go to lessons again.

It was around lunchtime that the mood changed.

'I guess we'll have to find a way to fill our days for a few months,' Katie said, with a nervous edge to her voice. 'I'm not sure how I'll cope without the routine.'

She had a point. It was routine that had kept me going. 'We'll be okay, I assured her. Our boys will make sure we don't forget what time to get up in the morning.'

Katie's dog, Bailey, loved nothing more than racing around the park with Reggie, and the feeling was mutual.

'True! That'll be an amazing way to spend our days.'

I was about to agree, when Frankie joined in. 'Don't think that I'm going to be spending all day following your dogs around the park. I want to spend some time with you before we have to make our Uni decisions.'

A sombre mood fell over our corner table in the Sixth Form café. Things were changing and we'd never be sitting here, all together, like this again. We had different exam timetables and would race home to revise after each one. None of us were confident that we had done enough to pass, let alone get the grades we needed.

'We've got our holiday to look forward to,' Maya reminded us, lightening the mood. 'My passport arrived yesterday, so I'm ready to go.'

'Shit. My passport,' I said, and promptly sent Mum a text to remind her that we still hadn't filled out the form.

'All we have to do is get these exams out the way and we can have the time of our lives,' Maya said, 'whether Dani joins us or not!'

'Thanks!' I exclaimed, vowing to get my passport form completed as soon as I got home. 'I'm not missing that holiday for anything.'

Fifty

It's done. It's over. My brain hurts.

Whoever came up with the idea that exams are the best way to measure whether I have learnt anything, needs to have a quite word with him or herself. All it has proved is that I had the stamina to stay awake all night while panic reading notes that didn't made sense and then been able to regurgitate it all the following day. If you asked me to answer those questions again now, I wouldn't be able to form words, let alone put them into sentences.

I heard most of my friends, and even Frankie, say, 'That was the worst two weeks of our lives.'

No, it wasn't! It was horrible, exhausting and painful in a lot of ways, but it definitely wasn't the worst two weeks of my life. Keeping some perspective helped me not to overthink every answer I wrote. I kept this up throughout each exam.

'What did you write for question three?' Frankie asked after one of the exams.

'I can't remember what question three was. It doesn't matter now, it's done,' I replied, surprising myself as much as Frankie.

'What have you done with Dani, you imposter,' she joked, and then turned to someone else and asked exactly the same question, embarking on a deep analysis of whether she would get any marks for what she had written.

Usually, I'd be doing the same thing, worrying about what I'd written and over-analysing every aspect of every answer I'd given. It wasn't that I didn't care, far from it. Standing outside the exam hall after that final exam, I took a deep breath and not only felt grateful that it was over, but I felt grateful that I could honestly say, 'I did my best.'

And I did. I'm sure there were days that I could have worked harder and I know that there were days that I spent with Frankie that were supposed to have been scheduled revision days, but I promised myself that I would concentrate on more than just the exams. I think that was what helped me. I still made sure I was training, still saw my friends and I went out in the fresh air with Reggie twice a day, making sure I had my happiness fix. Doing those things helped me, they didn't get in the way of revision, they made revision easier.

Training worked my brain and body, and quite often, I found it much easier to get into revision after I had been to taekwondo. I had physically worked through all of my nervous energy and by the time I was back at home, I was feeling chilled out about the exams and was happily reading, rather than trying to read in a panic, like the night before an exam.

Seeing my friends was also a mixed experience. It was amazing to hang out and have a laugh, but we'd always end up talking about the exams and I usually came home in more of a panic than when I'd left. Having a super smart friend like Katie meant that I always felt a little bit inferior in the brains department. I suppose that also made me work harder, so it wasn't always a bad thing.

If it wasn't for Reggie, I would definitely have gone insane. Getting out with him in the mornings meant I had to get up and dressed. It was still quite early by the time we were home and I felt ready to be productive. If I hadn't taken him out, I would have stayed in bed and it would have taken me ages to motivate myself to get dressed and start revising. He also gave me the perfect excuse to work to a deadline. He loved his lunchtime half an hour of playing in the garden, so that was my first deadline and he was very helpful when I made lunch. Then, we had the second deadline of his evening walk. If I made it through my planned revision, we had even longer in the park, which was a win-win for us both. I don't think that sitting at my desk for extra hours staring at my notes would have been a better use of my time.

So, I can now say for sure, 'I did my best,' and that's enough for me. I know I'll be shitting myself when results day comes around, but for now, I'm okay.

I have some time to get used the idea that I never have to go back to Sixth Form. That's a strange feeling. I'm now feeling drained after the last exam.

'What are you going to do with yourself now?' Mum asks, seeing me staring into space.

'Sleep,' I answer, but know that isn't enough. 'I want look for a job to start saving some money for our holiday, and for Uni,' I quickly add.

'That sounds like a brilliant idea,' Mum says.

She has been amazing and hasn't put any pressure on me to pay for stuff, but I want to be able to earn some money for myself. I'll be paying off a student loan until the day I die, at least that's what it feels like, so I need to do something to earn money.

'I'll start looking tomorrow,' I say, feeling quite excited about a new challenge already. 'First, I need to go and get ready to punch things.'

Driving to taekwondo, I feel a rush of excitement. I am driving a car, having passed my test first time. I have finished all of my exams and even though there's always nerves around results, I am confident that I had done enough to get into Uni. I am starting to work towards my black belt, something that I have dreamed of for years and I am about to go on my first holiday with a group of amazing friends and a wonderful girlfriend. Does life get any better than this?

Walking into training I am greeted by my instructor. 'You're smiling. I take it the exams are over? What're you doing with yourself now?' he asks.

'I'm just starting to figure that out,' I tell him, joking as I add, 'If only I could be paid to punch things.'

He laughs, 'Be careful what you wish for, Dani.'

I have no idea what he means, but it doesn't matter. Tonight, I am focusing on the big black belt dream and nothing else.

Fifty-One

Frankie has been talking non-stop about the Uni she's going to. She's lucky, she's had a letter offering her an unconditional place because she came in the top three at a cross-country running event.

'They know I'll win medals for their team,' she said earlier today at her house, buzzing that she no longer had to worry about her exam results. 'I wish I'd known before the exams, but I just can't wait to move out and start a new adventure. You'll only be a short train ride away no matter which Uni you go to.'

It was brilliant to hear Frankie so excited about it all, but I was starting to get nervous that she'd love her new life so much that she'd forget about me. We'd been sheltered here, living in a Sixth Form bubble without much else going on in our lives. Frankie couldn't wait for Fresher's Week, was ready to join loads of clubs and make new friends. I felt sick at the thought of starting again somewhere new. I'd done it twice in three years and just as I'd started to feel happy and settled, it had been time to move on again.

'Things will be different, but it doesn't change how I feel about you,' she told me softly. 'We'll be able to visit each other and make the most of the time we have together, without our parents getting in the way.'

'What if I stay here?' I asked, knowing that Frankie disapproved as she thought it was time for me to go and have a new adventure. She laughed when I first told her that I was thinking about staying at home so I hadn't mentioned it again.

'I thought you were waiting for your results to make sure you could get on the best course?' She sounded surprised that I was still considering staying at home, like it should be a backup plan if I didn't get the grades, but definitely not a first choice.

'I'm still thinking about all the options and I don't want to be paying back a loan until the day I die.' I knew that mentioning money made more sense to Frankie than admitting I was scared at the thought of moving out.

'I wish we could go to the same Uni,' she whined.

'Not that again!' I had run out of things to say about it. We were trying to be sensible and focusing on what we wanted to do with our lives, not just finding somewhere that would be a second best for both of us.

My phone rang. 'Saved by the bell, now you don't have to listen to me wishing we could spend more time together.'

Ignoring Frankie's comment, I answered it.

'Dani, do you have a minute?'

'Of course, is something wrong?' It was my taekwondo instructor. I had no idea why he'd call me if something was wrong, but I had literally never received a call from him before.

'Just a heads up. We are about to advertise a new job and I wanted you to know about it before you decide about which Uni to go to.'

I could feel my heart starting to race. A job? A taekwondo job?

'It's not a lot of money and it's not full time, so if you were interested in applying we'd be able to work your hours around Uni. But you'd need to be local. We're running some community projects, and some youth projects and we're looking to train up a youth mentor to join the team. So, would you like me to send you the information?'

'Yes, totally, yes please, that sounds like a dream come true. I mean, I know I'd have to apply, but totally yes, yes please, yes.'

'Thought you'd say that.' Laughing, he rang off and I immediately started clicking the refresh button on my emails.

'Who's made your dreams come true?' asked Frankie.

Still ignoring her shift in mood, I told her. 'This could be the most amazing opportunity,' I screamed, feeling overwhelmed with excitement. 'I could get paid to be doing taekwondo and be getting great experience for being a Sports Psychologist too.'

'It also means you'd have the perfect excuse to stay here.'

Ouch. She really knew how to burst the bubble. 'I'm going home. I need to work on my application.' I didn't feel like it gave me an excuse. I felt like it gave me a reason. I refused to let Frankie's dream of moving away cloud my own dream of staying safe and happy, having worked so hard to get to where I was. If she couldn't understand that, then maybe it was for the best we had decided to apply to different universities.

'What's got into you?' Mum shouted as I burst through the door and sprinted upstairs to get my laptop.

'You won't believe what just happened,' I shouted back.

'I don't think that could be any more perfect,' Mum said, when I told her about the job. 'It is as if they wrote it with you in mind.'

'I hope they did!'

'You know that you have my full support on this, Dani.'

'It would mean I'd be staying here,' I said, knowing that Mum had already said it would be okay to stay. 'Do you think I should leave the application and focus on getting my results and then deciding about where to go?' The excitement had turned to fear. Would this mean I had sealed my fate and that I would be staying at home for another three years rather than taking a risk and moving out?

'Dani, I mean this with love. At the moment, the choice isn't yours. They haven't offered you the job. They've only asked if you'd like to apply. If you get offered the job, then you can start thinking about the options, but you have to apply first.'

That was a fair point! I knew that at the very least, I wanted to be in with a chance of getting the job, so first things first.

It was time to fill in my first job application.

Fifty-Two

'Soz. Again! x,' came another message from Frankie last night.

I wasn't sure if I wanted to talk to her but when she called I knew I couldn't ignore her either.

'You're just so confident in going for your dreams and I don't want you to leave me because I'm an immature loser,' she said.

I was not expecting that. Frankie thought I was confident? She was worried about me leaving her? Wow.

'I'm terrified,' I admitted to her. 'I don't know what to do for the best, I'm trying to figure it all out and I don't want you to leave me because I'm boring and still living with my mum.'

There was silence as we realised we were both frightened of the same thing. Change. Things were changing and the excitement of leaving Sixth Form was overwhelming because we didn't know what would happen next. We didn't know if we could manage being apart. We didn't know what to do for the best.

'Are you definitely staying at home?' Frankie asked. This time, there was genuine interest in her voice.

'Yeah, I am.' Saying it out loud for the first time was a relief. 'I know I might always wonder whether I would've enjoyed living in Halls, but this way, I get the best of everything.'

'You're right. You get someone to do your washing, cook you nice meals and still get to go and live the Uni lifestyle whenever you want.'

I felt the need to defend myself even though we both knew it wasn't true. 'You know I do my share around the house! It's the only reason Mum's letting me stay.'

Writing my application last night, it became obvious to me that I couldn't leave. More than that, I didn't want to leave.

It's not about being frightened of moving away, it's about

making a conscious decision to stay. My friends are moving away, they're all going off to Uni and Callie is still on her mission to be a global superstar, so I know I'll be starting again with meeting new people. Once I decided I was staying here, I started to feel excited about that.

I want to have a new adventure, I want to meet new people and I definitely want to enjoy Uni. I just don't want those things at the expense of everything else that matters to me.

I have learnt the hard way that moving away doesn't necessarily make everything better. It isn't always a new adventure. I wouldn't change what I have now, but the journey to get here has taught me more than I ever wanted to know about valuing what you have, not taking it for granted and being grateful for the amazing things that happen every day. After all, that's all any of us have. This moment right now.

In my application, I was asked about how I believed I could be a positive role model to the young people I would be working with.

I wrote, 'I understand first-hand what it is like to feel profound fear, to succumb to the dark days and to feel like there's no hope. I don't underestimate the pain that someone feels when they are experiencing their own dark days and I don't believe there's an easy way out. Being honest about that shows young people that their feelings are valid and necessary. We don't all have to be happy all of the time, but there are choices that we can make to help us along the way. I have been on both sides of those choices. Sometimes I haven't made a decision to help myself, sometimes I have decided to hide away. Sometimes I have chosen to do the opposite, and for me, taekwondo has been a significant part of making those positive choices. I haven't always trained as hard as I could, I have missed some sessions and maybe if I had worked harder, I'd already be wearing my black belt. I can, however, share the message that it's the small choices, each and every day, that make the difference. I can share that message, along with my own journey of surviving, in a way that offers hope to the people who join the community programmes.'

I cried as I wrote it. I have never seen myself as a role model, but I guess we're all role models in one way or another. I've had people around me to help me when I needed it the most and I know that not everyone is that lucky. Maybe I can help to change that.

Pressing 'send' last night, desperately hoping that I would be offered the job and with Reggie's head resting on my knee, I'd known that there wasn't a choice. My life is here, for now, and I'm excited about that. My friends will come back and visit and I can drive to see them if they invite me. Mum's happy for me to stay and Frankie keeps saying we're more like housemates than mum and daughter. I think she's right. I even have a relaxed relationship with Sammy now and at least I'll have someone right here who can fix my laptop.

I hope things work out with Frankie. She makes me happy. We have our holiday with the girls to look forward to before we have to think about her moving away, and that is something I am definitely looking forward to.

Life is good. I am forever grateful that I can say that and mean it. It's been a rollercoaster, that's for sure, but with my best friend by my side, dribbling on my knee, I know I'm ready for whatever comes next.

Reggie & Me

Marie Yates

(Lodestone Books, 978-1-78279-723-4)

FINALIST WINTER 2014/2015 THE PEOPLE'S BOOK PRIZE

Reggie & Me is the first book in the *Dani Moore Trilogy*. Dani's story is told through her diary in the wake of her rape and subsequent court case.

Having moved with her mum, Dani starts Year Eleven at a new school, facing various challenges that bring a renewed energy to face whatever is thrown at her and to carry on regardless. She realises that 'normality' is something that she can define herself, with the help of her dog Reggie and the people around her.

Reggie & Me is more than a story of survival, as the reader is taken on an inspiring journey of personal development, interweaved with tools that girls and young women can use to create the positive future they deserve.

Sammy & Me

Marie Yates

(Lodestone Books, 978-1-78535-502-8)

Dani Moore, a teenage rape survivor, embarks upon the next phase in her life as she starts Sixth Form College. She hopes that this will be the new start she has been desperate for, having had a difficult final year at school. With an unwelcome change at home, her friends busy with their own lives and difficult reminders of her past, Dani wonders where she can turn for help. With her rescue dog, Reggie, by her side and a lifeline in the form of a new friend, will Dani make it through another rollercoaster year?

Sammy & Me is the second book in the *Dani Moore Trilogy*.

About the Author

Marie Yates is a writer, speaker and social entrepreneur. She is a Director of Canine Perspective CIC, a social enterprise which was established due to the success of Reggie and Me. Marie's passion for working with survivors and rescue dogs has created a global legacy utilising the human-canine bond.

LODESTONE BOOKS

Lodestone Books
YOUNG ADULT FICTION

Lodestone Books offers a broad spectrum of subjects in YA/NA literature. Compelling reading, the Teen/Young/New Adult reader is sure to find something edgy, enticing and innovative. From dystopian societies, through a whole range of fantasy, horror, science fiction and paranormal fiction, all the way to the other end of the sphere, historical drama, steam-punk adventure, and everything in between (including crime, coming of age and contemporary romance). Whatever your preference you will discover it here.

If you have enjoyed this book, why not tell other readers by posting a review on your preferred book site. Recent bestsellers from Lodestone Books are:

AlphaNumeric

Nicolas Forzy

When dyslexic teenager Stu accidentally transports himself into a world populated by living numbers and letters, his arrival triggers a prophecy that pulls two rival communities into war.

Paperback: 978-1-78279-506-3 ebook: 978-1-78279-505-6

Shanti and the Magic Mandala

F.T. Camargo

In this award-winning YA novel, six teenagers from around the world gather for a frantic chase across Peru, in search of a sacred object that can stop The Black Magicians' final plan.

Paperback: 978-1-78279-500-1 ebook: 978-1-78279-499-8

Time Sphere

A timepathway book

M.C. Morison

When a teenage priestess in Ancient Egypt connects with a schoolboy on a visit to the British Museum, they each come under threat as they search for Time's Key.

Paperback: 978-1-78279-330-4 ebook: 978-1-78279-329-8

Bird Without Wings

FAEBLES

Cally Pepper

Sixteen-year-old Scarlett has had more than her fair share of problems, but nothing prepares her for the day she discovers she's growing wings...

Paperback: 978-1-78099-902-9 ebook: 978-1-78099-901-2

Briar Blackwood's Grimmest of Fairytales

Timothy Roderick

After discovering she is the fabled Sleeping Beauty, a brooding goth-girl races against time to undo her deadly fate.

Paperback: 978-1-78279-922-1 ebook: 978-1-78279-923-8

Escape from the Past

The Duke's Wrath

Annette Oppenlander

Trying out an experimental computer game, a fifteen-year-old boy unwittingly time-travels to medieval Germany where he must not only survive but figure out a way home.

Paperback: 978-1-84694-973-9 ebook: 978-1-78535-002-3

Holding On and Letting Go

K.A. Coleman

When her little brother died, Emerson's life came crashing down around her. Now she's back home and her friends want to help, but can Emerson fight to re-enter the world she abandoned?

Paperback: 978-1-78279-577-3 ebook: 978-1-78279-576-6

Midnight Meanders

Annika Jensen

As William journeys through his own mind, revelations are made, relationships are broken and restored, and a faith that once seemed extinct is renewed.

Paperback: 978-1-78279-412-7 ebook: 978-1-78279-411-0

Reggie & Me

The First Book in the Dani Moore Trilogy

Marie Yates

The first book in the Dani Moore Trilogy, *Reggie & Me* explores a teenager's search for normalcy in the aftermath of rape.

Paperback: 978-1-78279-723-4 ebook: 978-1-78279-722-7

Unconditional

Kelly Lawrence

She's in love with a boy from the wrong side of town...

Paperback: 978-1-78279-394-6 ebook: 978-1-78279-393-9

Readers of ebooks can buy or view any of these bestsellers by clicking on the live link in the title. Most titles are published in paperback and as an ebook. Paperbacks are available in traditional bookshops. Both print and ebook formats are available online.

Find more titles and sign up to our readers' newsletter at http://www.johnhuntpublishing.com/children-and-young-adult

Follow us on Facebook at https://www.facebook.com/JHPChildren and Twitter at https://twitter.com/JHPChildren